WIMBLEDON COMMON

Compiled & edited by
Ben Thomas & D. Kershaw

Wimbledon Common title is
Copyright © 2022 Black Hare Press
First published in Australia in November 2022 by Black Hare Press

The authors of the individual stories retain the copyright of the works featured in this anthology

All characters and events in this publication, other than those clearly in the public domain, are fictitious and any resemblance to real persons, living or dead, is purely coincidental.

All rights reserved. No part of this production may be reproduced, stored in a retrieval system, or transmitted, in any form or by any means, electronic, mechanical, photocopying, recording or otherwise, without the prior permission of the publisher and copyright owner.

Compilation, Editing and Formatting
Ben Thomas
D. Kershaw
S. Jade Path

Cover Design
Dawn Burdett

Jodie Angell
Karen Bayly
Christy Brown
Dawn Burdett
Maggie D. Brace
Tracy Davidson
Dawn DeBraal
D.J. Elton
Megan Feehley
J.W. Garrett
Gabby Gilliam
Rachel Ginsburg
Henry Herz
Kevin Hopson
L.N. Hunter
Isabelle Johnson
Stephen Johnson
Blaise Langlois
Steven Lord
Kayleigh Maddocks
Laura Nettles
Carl Papa Palmer
Leanbh Pearson
Lynne Phillips
Hazel Ragaire
N.E. Rule
A.H. Syme
D.J. Tyrer

The moonlight fades from flower and tree,
And the stars dim one by one;
The tale is told, the song is sung,
And the Fairy feast is done.
The night-wind rocks the sleeping flowers,
And sings to them, soft and low.
The early birds erelong will wake:
'Tis time for the Elves to go.

O'er the sleeping earth we silently pass,
Unseen by mortal eye,
And send sweet dreams, as we lightly float
Through the quiet moonlit sky;
For the stars' soft eyes alone may see,
And the flowers alone may know,
The feasts we hold, the tales we tell:
So 'tis time for the Elves to go.

From bird, and blossom, and bee,
We learn the lessons they teach;
And seek, by kindly deeds, to win
A loving friend in each.
And though unseen on earth we dwell,
Sweet voices whisper low,
And gentle hearts most joyously greet
The Elves where'er they go.

When next we meet in the Fairy dell,
May the silver moon's soft light
Shine then on faces gay as now,
And Elfin hearts as light.
Now spread each wing, for the eastern sky
With sunlight soon will glow.
The morning star shall light us home:
Farewell! for the Elves must go...

—Louisa May Alcott, "Fairy Song"

Table of Contents

Perkins' Short Guide to the Beasts of Wimbledon Common

by Kayleigh Maddocks

Hello, dear reader. My name is Persephone Perkins, and this is my guide to the beasts and creatures that reside on Wimbledon Common, compiled after many years of study and observation. Whilst the human population remains sceptical of the magical animals that roam not just in woods and parks, but in our own back gardens, my aim is to dispel the myths and silence the naysayers.

Chupacabra

Originally indigenous to South America, the singular Chupacabra (lovingly referred to as Chups by rangers) who lives on the Common, was released in an ill-fated attempt to control the imp population. Rather than hunt down its intended prey, Chups has focused on eating the native fauna, including badgers and weasels. Reader, be warned: beneath the adorable nickname lies sharp teeth and claws that can eviscerate a family of four in seconds.

Dragons

Whilst dragon populations have decreased worldwide during the last century, largely due to deforestation and devastation of their natural habitat, the Common is home to at least two breeds; the English Sidesplitter and the rarer Golden variety. Dragons commonly hibernate underground for the winter, emerging in early to mid-spring, and will not seek out humans. However, in recent years, they have turned several illegal hunting parties to ash.

Dwarves

Normally mountain-dwelling folk, the Common's dwarves' relocation to Wimbledon was part of larger plans to introduce the species to the United Kingdom. Measuring at just under two feet tall, the miniature community continues to thrive, though care should be taken on approach to the dwarf village nestled neatly behind the Putney Common. Live demonstrations of dwarven craftmanship are scheduled weekly, and trinkets can be purchased at the annual festive fayre.

Fairies

Arguably the pest of the Common, Fairies are a relatively new, invasive species. There has been some debate about who introduced them to the Common, but it is agreed that their sudden appearance during the 1980s was likely accidental. They can often be observed around water sources and after heavy rain, though they should never be approached, for as adorable as they may seem, they can skin a small animal in the blink of an eye. Whilst no human fatalities have been attributed to them, they have a pack mentality, and several severe attacks have been recorded.

&oblins

Goblins are commonplace in most woods and fields of England; however, the Wimbledon variety are known particularly for their greediness. Be warned, any trinkets or treasures left by those spending an afternoon leisurely strolling across the green will be promptly snatched up as the sun falls. Ranging in height from two to four feet, like most of the beasties that roam the Common, Goblins are primarily nocturnal and will only be seen during the day if their hidey-holes are disturbed by pesky humans.

Hidebehind

Have you ever had the feeling that *something* is watching you? Something lurking in the shadows in the corner of the room, or hiding under the bed? The thing that makes you want to run up the stairs as fast as you can once you turn off the light. Then you've probably encountered a Hidebehind! As the name suggests, these beasts attempt to conceal themselves from the line of direct sight, normally hiding behind felled trunks in Fishpond Wood. Excellent stalkers with a penchant for disembowelling, the Hidebehind is a silent yet deadly predator—and, as such, traversing the woods is ill-advised after dark.

Hoblots

Possibly the most elusive of all who have made the Common their home, the Hoblots have also taken on the role of its guardians. Due to their expert shapeshifting ability, many of us fortunate enough to frequent the Common have probably passed one or two without even knowing. Whilst the reclusive nature of these creatures leaves great gaps in the available literature, it is believed they live near the Windmill, and on breezy days if you try hard (and there's enough goodness in your heart) you may be lucky enough to catch a glimpse of a Hoblot keeping watch.

Imps

Several fruitless attempts have been made to control the imp population (*see Chupacabra*). These mischievous beasties may seem fun and harmless, but this ugly cousin of the fairy can often trick the unsuspecting visitor into perilous situations. Whilst some believe imps are demons sent from a hell dimension, the Common population was originally sourced in Sussex.

Kerplimes

When reports were first made of small, subterranean creatures promenading the Common with squirming umbrellas (*see Land Shark*), the Common's rangers were quick to ban mushroom picking. Their existence was later proved, however, when photographic evidence was captured by local children on a school trip. Rarely seen above ground due to their upside-down noses (even the smallest amount of rain can prove fatal), they may be observed during the dry season hunting for Land Sharks.

Land Shark

Larger and less deadly than their aquatic cousins (to humans, anyway), Land Sharks have evolved to breathe air. Another notable difference is the stone-like growths that adorn their fins, allowing them to both move across rock and through sand with ease, but also to be more attuned to the movement and vibrations of the earth. Whilst they are cunning yet grumpy in nature, Land Sharks are eternally hunted by their mortal enemies to be used as living umbrellas (*see Kerplimes)*. Whilst Common rangers receive many a report regarding concern for the Land Shark's welfare, fear not—they typically free themselves after a short period of time, snacking on their captor as a reward for their patience.

Leshyie

Brought over as saplings from Croatia in the early 1960s, the Common boasts a thriving orchard of Leshyie. A humanoid tree, Leshyie feature deer-like antlers that can pierce the skin of person and animal alike. Once renown for abducting children cursed by relatives, every Wimbledon Leshy is more tolerant of humans than their ancestors. However, whilst every effort is taken each year to prune the more hostile of the grove, the rangers take no responsibility when parents choose to curse out their children—jokingly, or otherwise—within earshot.

Lunasplotches

Every eight months, the Common plays host to the Lunasplotches—an alien race from a moon behind Saturn. Covering their green-and-purple-splotched, blue skin with robes, their grasp of the English language is a little muddled, and they often speak many words backwards. The Common webpage lists the next decade's worth of planned Lunasplotch camping expeditions, and human visitors are reminded to follow first contact protocols.

Nightmare

The Nightmare is a curious beast, taking on a unique form for whoever stumbles across its path, usually of—you've guessed it—their worst nightmare. When hunting, the Nightmare can rage for upwards of five to seven days, tormenting and terrifying its victims, in some circumstances, to death. As it feeds on fear, my only advice for those facing the Nightmare is to run. Fast. The rangers keep the Commons website up-to-date with an estimate of when the Nightmare is likely to wake from its hibernation (usually every five to ten years) and nighttime visitors are requested

to check this before setting off.

Puppet Men

Has your friend been acting strangely? Maybe they still look the same, yet something is *off.* They're moving differently—like they are suspended on strings, and there's *nothing* behind the eyes. Well, I have an answer for you, but I can guarantee you won't like it—they've likely been taken over by a Puppet Man. Known for capturing unsuspecting children and adults, the Puppet Men are a terrifying species known to eat their victim's brains and take over their bodies. Visitors beware.

The Bog Child

Normally appearing when the sun rises or sets, this bog-dwelling monster takes on the form of a child, crying to get the attention of its unsuspecting victims. Gifted with the ability to change a person's reality, the Bog Child tricks people into escorting it to its home, which is little more than planks floating on water. Very few people who have met the Bog Child have survived to share their accounts. An endangered species, there are only fifty Bog Children left in the wild.

The Bog Hag

Another inhabitant of the swamplands, Bog Hags are expert shapeshifters who can fit their form to both human and fae. The marshy terrain of the bogs is traversed effortlessly by the Bog Hags, who also possess the ability to breathe underwater. Little else is known about this resident of the Common due to the fatal nature of all encounters.

The Plant Woman

A shapeshifter—when hunting, the Plant Woman will peel off her face and wig. Beneath the bark ribbons lies her true form; a pod (which was once her dark green skull) and a mass of sticky green leaves, adorned with red wet hairs that stick out in all directions. If that wasn't enough nightmare fuel, the pod can split itself open, revealing a giant mouth filled with goo-dripping teeth, Arguably the most terrifying looking of all the Common's creatures, the Plant Woman should be avoided by all children who do not wish to be used as fertiliser.

The Thing That Lives in the Pond

Whilst open water swimming in any of the Wimbledon Common ponds is discouraged, extreme caution should be taken by anyone who attempts to dip a toe in the Queensmere pond. Once the site of duelling Victorians, Queensmere is rumoured to house the *Thing That Lives in the Pond*. Whilst not the most imaginative name, no one who has faced the *Thing* has lived long enough to share any interesting details about it.

Trolls

Believed to have been introduced to southern England during the Norse invasion, the Common's current troll population has been settled since the time of King Harald. These terrifying, long-limbed, and always ravenous, creatures can be found in the woodland. Visitors should remain wary when in these areas as despite their size, a troll can close the gap between themselves and their dinner quickly.

Unicorns

Originally a gift to Queen Victoria, Wimbledon's award-winning Unicorn herd are stabled in the village in winter months but are given free-range of the Common between spring and autumn. Whilst a beautiful and rare sight, humans are warned against approaching the Unicorns, especially during breeding season (May until August), as they can be unpredictable and feisty, packing a mighty kick.

Weens

Timid and mysterious, the Common's singular ween prefers the solitude of the depths of the earth, surfacing only when they run out of the one thing they cannot live without—sweets! Eagle-eyed guests may spot the ween scamping around on All Hallows' Eve amongst the crowds of costumed children, exploring local houses for candied goodness. Sadly, weens top the endangered magical species list, and the Common boasts one of, if not *the* last of these ancient child-sized creatures.

Witches

Whilst not permanent inhabitants of the Common, as many now live and thrive within our own communities, Witches hold many events throughout the calendar year—from monthly full moon celebrations to Beltane, Samhain, and Yule. Mortals are reminded that whilst most events are human-friendly, the annual Vampire Ball, held on the third Thursday in November, is not appropriate for those with a beating heart.

Wisps

The Common's Wisps largely stay around bodies of water, primarily the bog on the southern border. Largely harmless, the Wisps will attempt to lure unsuspecting visitors into the lakes, misleading them by presenting as brightly coloured orbs. This past year marked the highest level of people requiring rescue from the ponds, most of whom were tempted in by Wisps.

Zombie Fairies

Visitors to the Common should take care when

traversing areas concealed by leaves as not to disturb Zombie fairies. Thought by many to be little more than a tale to scare children, this rare yet aggressive sub-species has been known to behead their playmates. If you're unlucky enough to hear the terrifying shrill call of a zombie fairy, my only advice is to clamp your hands over your ears and run for safety.

Afterword

Whilst the Common is a wonderful place, teeming with an array of beautiful yet dangerous, creatures, I advise you, reader, against the seductive tug of temptation. Whilst you may feel pulled to pet a unicorn, capture an imp, or witness a Leshy firsthand, one must always be aware of the risks.

Or you may never return from your visit to Wimbledon Common.

A mother of four, **Kayleigh Maddocks** thought the pandemic would be the best time to start writing. She finds escape in building worlds and playing with magic.

The Wimbledon Witches' Fete
by Karen Bayly

melia Smythington-Hope, age eight, didn't intend to be kidnapped.

Yet just minutes ago, George Rotter had grabbed her from her bed and shoved her inside a large blue duffle bag, then hitched it over his shoulder.

George wanted payback. Yesterday, Amelia's father, head of Big Bank, had repossessed his mother's home. A loving son, he intended to ransom the girl for the house. He thought his victim would be scared and had expected tears. Nothing prepared him for the bagful of spite in his hands.

"Help! Let me out, you scum-sucking bottom feeder. Wait until my daddy finds out. He spits on stinky subhumans like you!"

The bag shifted, throwing him off balance as the little miss kicked and pounded her fists against his back.

"Stop wriggling and shut yer mouth."

"Don't you tell me to keep quiet. You're a wicked man!"

Thank heavens the Smythington-Hope house stood close to Wimbledon Common, for it presented the best route to where he'd parked his van. He couldn't get there soon enough.

He veered off the pathway and ducked through a copse. When he emerged on the other side, he paused. What he should have seen was an expanse of grass, lit by moonlight. What he saw instead were dozens of colourful stalls and tents, aglow with tiny stars and moons, orbiting the grounds like a mini universe. And the visitors! Some were men and women, but others appeared to be animals, trotting around on their hind legs, buying fairy floss served by real fairies, and searching for bargains.

To his left stood a stage decorated with silk banners held up by the gossamer webs of silver spiders. To his right, a pair of women in long purple and black dresses floated past on broomsticks. One nodded at him, and the other smiled. He blushed.

"Aren't they entrancing? Our Siren Sisters are a big hit with our male customers."

George almost dropped Amelia. In front of him stood a tall woman with bright red hair, holding out her hand.

"I'm Aubrilla Dartmouth, this year's organiser of the Wimbledon Witches' Fete. And who might you be?"

"G-George Rotter."

"I see. And who is in the bag?"

"Me! Amelia Smythington-Hope. Help me. Daddy will make it worth your while."

"Ah." The red-haired witch stared at George in a way that made his heart pound with fear. "We don't approve of kidnapping, Mr Rotter. Despite a reputation for abducting children, witches actually care for the young ones. We only steal those who need stealing. And we never eat them. Can you say the same?"

"N-never ate a child in my life, Ms…?" He gulped.

"Dartmouth. And I meant, did Amelia need stealing?"

"Probably, Ms Dartmouth. She's feisty, which ain't a bad

thing, but she's a rude, stuck up little—"

"And were you going to teach her a lesson? I will know if you aren't telling the truth."

She clicked her fingers and an iron dagger appeared in the air, pointing straight at George's heart.

"N-no, Ms Dartmouth. Her dad stole my mam's home, and I wanted to make him give it back."

"Hm. That won't do, Mr Rotter. I must insist you hand her over to me."

"But, my mam—"

"I sympathise, but this isn't the way to deal with it."

He eyed the dagger. "Oh, all right. It's not working out, anyway."

Sighing, he placed the duffle bag on the ground and unzipped it. Amelia scrambled out and aimed a punch at George's face, but her fist froze in mid-air. Try as she might, it wouldn't move forward.

The witch frowned. "Violence is unacceptable, young lady. Now George, I'm a reasonable woman, so I'll make you an offer. Pledge to be my servant until the next Wimbledon Witches' Fete, and I will make sure your mother gets her house back tomorrow."

Amelia stamped her foot. "You're letting him get away with kidnapping me?"

Aubrilla spun around, fierce sparks of energy haloing her head. "You need to learn humility, girl!"

The young miss opened her mouth to speak, but a spell blocked her words. The witch turned back to George.

"Mr Rotter, do you agree with my terms?"

His knees were knocking so hard, he could barely answer.

"Yes, Ms Dartmouth, I do."

She clapped her hands once, then clicked her fingers twice. Amelia's eyes widened, and she trembled in fear. Where George once stood was a large black rat.

The witch scooped up Rat George and placed him on her shoulder.

"A lesson, Ms Smythington-Hope. Don't agree to anything without knowing the terms. Now, I'll get someone to take you around the fete. We have lots of wonderful things for children like *you* to see."

She leaned down and cradled Amelia's chin in her hand. "If I remove the silencing spell, do you think you can keep a civil tongue in your mouth?"

The young girl nodded. Out of the corner of her eye, she noticed the rat was weeping.

The witch ran her thumb over the girl's lips. "There now. All better. Say thank you."

"Thank you, Ms Dartmouth."

"And here comes Barnabas. I will leave you in his capable hands."

Amelia turned to find a large badger standing behind her. He wore a green waistcoat, red bow tie, and nothing else. He bowed.

"Good evening. I'm Barnabas Badger. Welcome to the annual Wimbledon Witches' Fete."

Amelia wasn't sure what to do or say, but she bobbed a curtsey remembered from ballet classes, and cleared her throat.

"Hello."

He offered her his arm.

"Shall I show you our wonderful stalls and entertainments?"

The normally plucky young girl was at a loss. No one had ever treated her with such politeness and grace. All she heard was criticism. "Amelia, you are better than that." Or,

"Amelia, stand up for yourself." Or, "Amelia, don't let them think you're weak." This was unusual and scary—but also exciting.

She looped her arm through his, willing to be guided. Barnaby smiled.

"First, a history lesson. The fete is the highlight of the witching year. It began in the 1600s. Each year, the witches choose a committee to run the event. It's a great honour to be chosen, but if anyone tries to influence that choice by magical or ordinary means, their peers ban them from attending for 150 years. Questions?"

"Wouldn't they be dead after 150 years?"

"Most probably. Few witches live longer than 140 years. But that's the point. Cheating is unfair, so cheaters must pay a price."

Amelia thought a punishment that ended after you'd died was overly harsh. But she wasn't a witch or even a grownup. Perhaps such punishments were usual. It was something to consider.

Barnabas tugged at her arm. "Now, come along. There is much to see and do."

Their first stop was a stall filled with glass objects. To

one side sat a large green ogre with four eyes on stalks who was blowing glass over an invisible fire. His left most eyeball swivelled toward them in greeting.

"Here we have Oliphas—a talented maker of magical ornaments. His work is much sought after by witches and wizards worldwide."

Barnabas continued talking, but Amelia no longer listened. A tiny, but elegant, unicorn had caught her eye. She touched it with one finger and it pranced on the spot, reflecting rainbows all over its surroundings.

She wanted it. Badly. But what could she use for money? Her guide was now chatting with the ogre. She double-checked neither were looking her way, then snatched the unicorn and hid it in her pyjama top pocket.

"Right, ready to move on?" The badger stood next to her, smiling. Had he seen what she'd done? If so, he was keeping it to himself.

Barnabas continued his nonstop talking as they toured. Amelia wanted to be entranced, but she felt odd, like something nasty lurked in her tummy. Still, a few things amused her.

There was Fizz Pop, a bright green sherbet that turned

you into a cartoon character complete with speech bubble. She'd smiled as other folk became animated creatures with the words "Bam!" or "Kapowie!" hanging over their heads, but declined to try it herself. Too afraid the stolen goods would fall out of her pocket.

Then there was the CryptoPuss, a cute little cat that changed colour, pattern, and texture to blend with its surroundings. Unfortunately, it made a farty sound when alarmed. Because people couldn't see it, they often sat on it by accident, so it frequently gave its farty alarm from under the person's backside. This had earned it the title of "Worst Pet Ever".

Usually, Amelia found fart noises hilarious, but this time she could not laugh. And that nastiness in her tummy had grown into something that wriggled and bumped. She didn't feel at all well.

Barnabas clapped his front paws together. "Ah, Amelia. You're in for a real treat! In a moment you will see Dr Zombo's Zinging Zorillas!"

They were back at the stage. Now thousands of tiny stars floated above it, casting a twinkling silvery light. People and animals pushed forward, eager to secure the best view.

With a flourish, the rear curtains opened, and four striped weasel-like creatures entered to thunderous applause. They took their positions, and a hush settled over the fete.

The one on the far left open his mouth and deep sounding *zing* filled the air.

"That's Zam," whispered Barnabas. "Then there's Zef, Zik, and Zotto. They're zorillas. Their song makes naughty children deathly ill with guilt worm. But that won't worry you, will it, Amelia?"

The next zorilla *zinged* a note higher than the first, followed by higher and higher *zings* from the remaining zorillas. The sound echoed in Amelia's head, and the world began to spin. She opened her mouth to vomit, and a large purple and yellow worm poked out its head.

Barnabas leaned over her. "Unwell, young lady? I wonder why that might be. Something you ate? Or something you *did?*"

His normally pleasant voice sounded harsh and unfriendly. When she looked up, he snarled at her. Behind him was the ogre, holding a large knife. To one side stood Aubrilla, eyes burning like coals. She grabbed Amelia by the neck of her pyjama top and lifted the girl's face to hers.

"We dislike children who steal from us, especially when we have been kind to them."

Amelia fumbled in her pocket and pulled out the unicorn. She offered it to the ogre.

"Here. I took it because I didn't know how to pay for it. I'm happy to give it back."

Oliphas smirked. "No returns. Want payment."

"But I have no money!"

"You have innocence. I make new unicorn with it. That what I take."

"No! Barnabas! Ms Dartmouth, save me!"

The badger shook his head. "There's nothing we can do, child. You stole from an ogre. You must answer to ogre law."

One of Oliphas's large green hands closed over her body and pressed her into the ground, while the other held a glass vial under her nose. She shivered and squirmed, her skin prickling as though hundreds of tiny ants crawled over her, nipping as they went. Her heart skipped two beats, then a pale pink vapour flowed from her nostrils. With each breath, her spirit sagged with the woes of the world. Her limbs were dead weights, and she realised her childhood was dying. Its loss was the saddest thing she'd ever experienced. She wished her entire life was over.

In a blur of black fur, Rat George leapt from Aubrilla's shoulder, sank a chiselled pair of teeth into the ogre's hand. Oliphas tried to shake the creature off, but the rat held fast, his jaws locked into flesh, his tiny claws piercing green skin. Enraged, the ogre grabbed his tormentor between thumb and forefinger and squeezed. George squeaked pitifully, then let go, falling to the ground. The ogre raised his foot to stomp the wee animal to death.

"Enough!" Aubrilla's voice sounded as though it came from someone ten times her size. "Murder is forbidden at this fete."

Oliphas snorted and tried to continue his horrible act, but the witch cast a stop motion spell. He could not move. Aubrilla swept forward and scooped up George.

"Are you all right, my dear?" She ran her fingers over him gently, letting sparks of healing energy fix his injuries. "There you are. You'll live. I look after my animals."

She turned on the ogre. "And you! I think your payment is complete. Unless you'd like me to fine you for hurting a witch's pet?"

Oliphas uttered a groan. He knew a witch fine was far worse than losing a glass unicorn.

"And you, Ms Smythington-Hope. The unicorn, please."

Amelia handed it over, suddenly glad to be rid of the cause of the troubles.

"Now, pick up that vial and breathe deeply."

She held the tiny bottle to her nose and inhaled. The pink vapour flowed upwards, tickling her nostrils as it spread into her lungs and from there into her blood and all over her body. Within seconds, she was herself again.

"Thank you ever so much, Ms Dartmouth."

"And now it's time for you to go home."

"Can I say goodbye to George first?"

"I thought you hated him."

"I did, but he saved my life."

She reached up and scratched Rat George gently under his chin.

"Thank you, and I'm sorry I caused you so much trouble."

He cuddled her finger with both paws, pressing his whiskery face against her skin.

Amelia bit her lip. Perhaps she could help him?

"Ms Dartmouth. Is there any chance you would turn George into a man today? I mean, I think he has shown he's a good person deep down, so a year as a rat seems unfair."

"I have made my decision, Ms Smythington-Hope. Don't push your luck. Now, home."

A myriad of red and green sparks crackled through the air, and Amelia closed her eyes. When she opened them again, she was in her own bed, and it was morning.

Amelia's life had changed since the Wimbledon Witches' Fete. She no longer acted like a spoiled brat. Her mother and father seemed happier too, and she understood how her dreadful behaviour had affected them. She now enjoyed school and liked being nice to people.

Today, her family was picnicking on Wimbledon Common. When she arrived, she hoped she'd see the witches' fete but, of course, it was no longer there. Having filled her tummy to bursting with yummy food, she decided to walk to the pond and feed the ducks while her parents finished their wine.

Out of the corner of her eye, she noticed a man. A

somewhat familiar fellow.

"George?"

"Hello, Amelia."

"You're not a rat anymore!"

"Because of you, Aubrilla undid the spell the next day. And me mam got her house back as well."

"I'm so glad. And thank you for my adventure. I learned a lot."

"Me too. Well, I'd better be off. Just wanted to say thanks."

With that, he hurried in the opposite direction. Amelia threw the remaining crumbs to the ducks and wandered back to her parents.

From the nearby copse, a pair of beady eyes, set in a pointy-nosed, black-and-white striped face, gazed at her and smiled.

Karen Bayly's passion for writing began as a child when she wrote soap operas for her dolls to perform. These days, her PhD in biology and her research background informs her writing, a fusion of realism, science, horror, and fantasy. Her work has appeared in *Yellow Mama Webzine, Black Petals Horror Magazine, and Every Day Fiction*. She has published one novel, *Fortitude*, and a novelette, *Tesato's Code*. She has stories appearing in anthologies from Black Hare Press, Black Beacon Press, and Crystal Lake Publishing. She lives in Sydney, Australia, with two cats, a guitar, and a ukulele.

Creatures of the Dark
by J.W. Garrett

Jade gazed at the sky as she sniffed the air. A storm was coming. She headed toward the tree line, shelter, and home. The only home she'd ever known. Her childhood memories were fuzzy. Her only clear recollections came after her arrival at Wimbledon Common about two years ago.

Folks tried to figure out her age, so Jade took the most common guess and confirmed it. "Yes," she answered the people's prying questions; now she was eleven. Sidestepping inquiries as to her parents with the flash of a glamour spell, Jade was well on her way home before the dumbfounded individuals gained their wits again. By then,

she would disappear into her beloved woodlands.

The only true guiding beacon in her world, Jade's magic, flowed as naturally as breathing. Rain spoke to her in heavy pitter-pats, and the wind whispered with a sway that brought to life the scents of the bog surrounding her, where all her special forest creatures thrived. The public knew little about the Common's unusual features. If the townsfolk ever found out, their fear would drive them to do terrible things.

As it was, the inky blackness of night brought forth its own judgment on a regular basis, managing the creature population, so the delicate balance between nature and its people never swung too far out of proportion. That way, each side, man and beast, might live in harmony.

A gnarled, ancient tree sprang from the earth, tramping deep into the forest, accompanying Jade on the half-mile hike to her home. The branches creaked and wobbled with the movement, leaves fluttering to the forest floor, where they'd begin a new journey of their own.

When her home came into view, the tree bark rippled and branches shivered a goodbye, before the giant guardian twisted and began its return trek, roots trailing behind.

"Thank you for the company." Ducking through the

undergrowth, past thorns and briars, to an enormous tree. Jade muttered a spell, and the tangled root system before her slithered aside, allowing her passage to the underground shelter where she lived with her animals. With another whispered enchantment, the roots and vines burrowed back into the earth.

Jade set to work preparing her potions, using the herbs and plants she'd gathered this morning. Under the watchful gaze of multiple creatures, Jade worked, casting spells, cooking and tasting her concoctions. Jade flicked her wrist, and while the empty glass bottles sucked in the brew, she spun to address the animals.

"Maybe this version of the elixir will work tonight." Jade sighed.

Victoria, the vampire bunny, flopped one ear down in agreement. Several glowing worms inched along, baring their teeth in their version of a hopeful smile.

"Come on now. I'll find something that helps…eventually." *If only speaking the words could make them true.* So far, she'd only avoided the deepest level of sleep about half the time. On other nights, all control was lost, and her mind, stuck in that dark place, created enchanted beings—regal, fire-breathing dragons. When that happened, her nightmares haunted her, then crossed over into the world of the living.

In a flurry of wings, three fae perched on her counter, clinging to the treasures that Jade had left for her friends under her tree. Sprinkling their faerie dust into the air, they muttered their own spells, then joined their friends. When night fully fell, they would all witness whether Jade would just sleep, or would visit the deepest recesses of her mind again.

She tilted the liquid to her lips and swallowed it down, all the animals gathering around her, like she might transform into something horrible. Who could blame them? "Go on now. Get busy. It'll be hours before I'll know if this latest version is working or not."

The day wore on, the busyness not distracting her thoughts from the looming evening and her efforts to cage what lived inside her.

When darkness chased away the last colours remaining of the sun, the animals scurried outside to feed, leaving only the fae with Jade. The spells they'd conjured brought calm to the space, but could they actually affect the outcome of the night? The fae flitted from place to place, suspended here and there, taking their pinpricks of light with them as they zigzagged across the room, the scattered pattern reflecting their anxious mood.

As was her usual evening ritual, Jade fought sleep, convinced that the mixture of spells had brought success this time. A cloud of thoughts fogged her mind, the flash of pictures crawling in behind. Jade slumped to the floor. A tendril of magic pierced the air, and the dream gripped her.

Dragon tongue slipped from her lips in the ancient summoning. The beasts roared a response.

They're coming…

Giant wings pummelled the air, whisper quiet in their graceful movements.

Flames ignited the inky blackness.

Bronze scales shimmered in the glow of their path, the wind shifting, redirecting, with the heavy sweep of their wings. The air heated with streaks of fire, painting red through the night.

Inside, the pixies spun their enchantments, attempting to wake Jade, but tonight was no different. Fated to be like all the rest. The cycle repeated as it always did. The forest animals blinked, eyes upturned to the disturbance cutting the sky, their hearts connected, beating out a frantic rhythm in answer to the dragons' calls.

Who would fulfil the primal curse?

The fae heaved a collective shaky breath and waited. They felt the gusts from the *swish* of dragons' wings; saw the beasts' belched smoke hanging in the air. Then the raised faces of the creatures caught glimpses of the dark images, rising higher and higher.

Inside, Jade dreamed on, whisking the dragons back to their own realm.

A tiny smile drifted to her lips. A new day awaited them. And for the first time…hope.

J.W. Garrett is a multi-award-winning author. Initiated into fantasy after reading *The Hobbit* in elementary school, she has been hooked ever since. She writes speculative fiction from the sunny beaches of Jacksonville, Florida, but loves the mountains of Virginia where she was born. Her writings include novels, short stories, and poetry. *Remeon's Legacy*, the final book in her fantasy series, Realms of Chaos, is out now. When she's not hanging out with her characters, her favourite activities are reading, running and spending time with family. www.jwgarrett.com.

Shrink Wrap
by N.E. Rule

Tabby brings the crisp bag to her open mouth, tilts her head back, and inhales the last of the crumbs. She might as well enjoy some treats before putting the shrink wrap to the test.

She hears the voice of the creepy janitor, Hilda, in her head. "Wrap your problem areas each night for only one hour at a time. After two weeks, you will be model-thin."

Earlier, Tabby's supposed BFF, Sophia, sat down at their regular lunch table as Tabby bit into a Galaxy bar.

"Hey, Flabby," Sophia greeted her, and all their friends laughed. Hilda was pushing a broom around their table and raised her eyebrows.

After lunch, Tabby decided to skip her Phys Ed class to avoid the changing room. When Tabby was the last to leave the cafeteria, Hilda approached her about a "magic" wrap.

"How do I know you didn't grab that out of the kitchen?" Tabby pointed to the box in question. It appeared to be a standard roll of cling wrap.

"I'm offering it to you for free. What do you have to lose?" Hilda cracked up at her own joke. The cackling set Tabby's teeth on edge.

"What's the catch?" Despite her scepticism, Tabby's pulse quickens in excitement. Hilda just shrugs with an impish grin.

Does she feel sorry for me? There were countless "Hilda the witch" rumours going around Wimbledon Common Prep School. Despite this, Tabby knows she will try anything if it might make her thinner.

When Tabby hears her dad snoring down the hall, she jams in the last Jaffa Cake then gets to it. She's delighted that the box reads "covers 30 metres." So, she starts down at her wide feet and rolls the cling wrap up and around each calf. She then works the plastic around her thighs, hips, and bum. Of course, she rolls twice around her muffin-top and jiggly chest. She then wraps her shoulders and pudgy neck, but then stops. Looking in the mirror at her full face staring back, she continues wrapping her whole head. Of course, she leaves a gap for her pert nose because she needs to breathe, and besides, it was always her best feature. She rips off two separate strips and wraps first her left arm and hand and then does her right.

She drops back onto the bed with an *oomph*. Her breathing is shallow due to the tight band around her chest and sounds ragged in her ears. The plastic heats and bubbles around her body, smelling like buttered toast. Sweat drips into her eyes, so she closes them.

The morning sun shines through the slit in her drapes and awakens her. She groans, feeling trapped beneath a dead weight pressing on her face, chest, and abdomen. Her bedroom door creaks open, but she can't see through the cling wrap plastered over her eyes. She blinks through the gauzy film., "Who's there? Dad?"

"Tabby?" She recognises Hilda's raspy voice.

"What are you doing in my house?" Tabby's voice comes out in a squeak. "Where's my dad?"

"I saw him leave for work, so I let myself in."

"Something feels wrong," Tabby whines.

"How long have you had this on?" Hilda *tsks*, tearing at the sheet of plastic wrap. "My instructions were for only an hour at a time."

Tabby feels a sharp pinch on her nose, and then she's rising. The plastic wrap falls away like a cloak. As Tabby lifts, she can't breathe. Finally, her nose is released, and she feels something solid under her feet. Glancing around her bedroom, she sees her furniture is now enormous. She has been placed on top of her dresser in front of the mirror.

Tabby stares in horror at her reflection. She has shrunk to half the size of a Barbie doll! Everything that is, except her nose, which is now a third the size of her body. "What have you done?" Tabby screeches and Hilda grimaces at her pitch, which is like that of yipping a chihuahua.

Tabby waddles back around, carrying the bottom of her nose in her arms like a pregnant woman holding her protruding belly. Tabby's eyes widen on Hilda, who is now

a giant in comparison.

"Fix me!" She screeches again. She lifts her leg to stomp her foot, but the weight of her nose imbalances her, so she falls onto her butt with a *thud*.

"Relax, I'm sure I have something." Hilda digs through her leather purse and pulls out a bottle of dark liquid. Opening it, she holds the dropper over the bridge of Tabby's nose and squeezes. There is a sizzling hiss as each drop hits Tabby's skin; a savoury smell of frying bacon permeates the room. She winces in pain but forces herself to sit still under the globules of brown goop.

Tabby starts to sneeze. With each sneeze, her nose shrinks in size until, finally, it's proportional to her face. With the weight off her chest, she sucks in a deep breath.

"There now, you're perfect." Hilda sniffs the air in satisfaction.

Tabby spins to look in the mirror and then turns back to Hilda. Her hands are flapping like she's doing a jazz dance; a brown glaze covers her body. "Are you kidding? You crazy witch! I'm still the size of a rat! Make me big again!" Tabby was yelling as loudly as her little lungs would allow.

Hilda scowls. "Bigger, smaller, thinner, taller—you kids

are never happy with your bodies!" Hilda raises her hand and pinches Tabby's shoulder and lifts her up. She carries her close to her own face as if doing an inspection. "You're the ideal size to me."

When Hilda's foul breath reaches Tabby's perfectly proportioned nose, Tabby gasps. She stares as Hilda gnashes her razor-sharp teeth.

"Put me down!" Tabby screams, kicking her feet frantically as she tries to wiggle free. But Hilda opens her mouth wider and drops Tabby in.

N.E. Rule attended Toronto Metropolitan University (TMU) for both creative writing and business communications. Her writing portfolio includes software specs, marketing copy, and training materials, however, her passion is fiction. The characters in her head are getting louder and refuse to wait for her spare time to come out and play.

The World You Cannot See
by Hazel Ragaire

Dear Human,

People might tell you that ancient trees do not exist in Wimbledon Common, and that's mostly true, but it is also a lie. That's just what humans' eyes tell them. Long ago, when humans had nearly destroyed us, the last of Wimbledon's original fairies worked together to make the most ancient tree in the Common invisible. You see, in every forest, one tree holds the magic of the place. That tree protects the life around it; it offers dens among its roots, homes within its trunk, and nests between its branches. Once, a thick forest blanketed Wimbledon Common boasting the most beautifully old and magic trees: oaks and alders and beeches and rowans and willows and chestnuts grew towards the sky reaching for the sun.

And my kin, the fairies of the forest, cared for those trees and the creatures they sheltered. The rowan trees were always my favourite, with their flame red berries with a five-pointed star on the bottom. I would eat them and squish them and dye my clothes with them; all the fairies came to me for beautifully coloured clothes. Don't tell anyone, but I always mixed a bit of blueberries into my rowan berries, so the colour turned out a deep, rich, lovely red.

Anyway, long, long ago, when humans moved from hunting in tribes to farming, they needed wood for houses and fences and more tools. They began chopping down the trees. But each tree fairy is bound to its own tree. When a sapling makes it to maturity and bears its first fruits, a fairy would appear to care for it. As long as the tree lives, so too does the fairy. Sadly, sometimes the trees died from disease or lightning strikes or insect damage. And when those trees' fairies died, we created a rhyme to remember their names and sung it often as we went about our daily tasks. This didn't happen very often. I mean, by the time I approached my 980th birthday, I'd memorised only thirty-six rhymes.

But when humans arrived, they would kill a tree and its fairy daily; sometimes a dozen trees and fairies would be cut down in a single day. This is why the sap of the alder flows red like blood. Sadness consumed the alders so much that when cut, they bleed for the loss of their fairies.

We lost a third of the forests when humans began farming.

Then came The Culling.

Humans eventually moved on to build towns and cities and needed the forest's wood to build. Men came into the old forests like plagues, culling them to nothing. Like locusts, they cut down everything they saw, leaving small branches littering the ground like bones. With all life comes magic— and when men separated a tree from its roots, the fairies turned to ash. Oblivious to the death they dealt, humans ravaged the forest. They killed nearly all the fairies in Wimbledon Common. The destruction didn't stop with the trees or the fairies; they killed our animal friends for food and fur: squirrels, foxes, rabbits, ferrets, all. Our magical forest transformed into a grassland graveyard, tree stumps polka-dotting as far as the eye could see: each stump a tombstone for a tree and its fairy. So many dead fairies, the dozen of us remaining couldn't remember the names of all the friends and family we'd lost. How can 12 remember thousands and thousands of names? We'd lost as many fairies as there are raindrops in a thunderstorm.

And so, the last of us gathered and put all our magic into protecting the ancient rowan tree in the centre of the Common. Its gnarly trunk had twisted and turned over the centuries, snaking around itself as it stretched and yearned towards the sky. Joining hands, we fluttered around the tree, summoning the most powerful magic we could through grief-stricken voices. We called out to the ancient magics and asked for protection of this tree; to conceal it from the eyes of men so the feathered and furred friends would have one last home among its ancient branches.

The magic came, but at a price.

The twelve of us lost our wings that day.

No longer could we float on breezes or fly through the air for the sheer joy of it.

We were no longer tied to a particular tree, and when the humans cut down the last visible trees we wept and raged. The next morning, we left.

On our tiny, tired feet we walked 471 days to find a new forest, not yet marred by humans. Ailsa, Briar, Cordela, Dash, Elowen, Magnus, Navi, the twins—Tansy and Titan—Wefan, Yin, and I gathered as many different tree seeds and berries and nuts as our enchanted pouches could hold. Gratefully accepting the hospitality of the fairies of that forest, we paused our return journey to rest and share our story. We urged the fairies to cloak their forest in invisibility to save themselves, their trees, and their furred and feathered friends. You may not know this, but fairies can't travel far beyond the bounds of their own forest. We urged the fairies to send messages with their beetles to other fairies in remaining forests to hide their forests as well. Thousands of remaining fairies all over the world sacrificed their wings to save Earth's most ancient trees and the forests they protected. And thus, sprites we became.

There are many things human eyes can't see; fairy forests are just one of them.

Over the centuries, we, the sprites of Wimbledon Common, rebuilt the forest. We cause mischief for humans whenever we can, well, because our memories are long, and

they took everything from us once. Sprites now, fae without wings, we work to rebuild our home. We've planted hundreds of new trees, and hundreds of new fairies grew from their magic. But there are more sprites than there should be.

It's a shame that human eyes will never see these trees; they are so old now some of them actually touch the clouds; their branches stretch across a mile. They house hundreds of creatures that once sought refuge, and the magic grants them safety and immortality within our hidden realm. Many creatures living in these trees are extinct in your world; while they are sad to stay within the protective boundary of the trees, they are happy to evade the human knives and arrows and guns. Perhaps one day if humans stop cutting down trees, we'll release our magic and you'll be able to see the world as it truly is and we won't need to hide it from you. But until then, know that there are worlds you cannot see: the sprites and fairies protect them from your kind.

Humans may call this a fantasy, but my kin calls it truth. Dare to believe in that which you cannot see. I leave this for you to find. Know every story has two sides. Humans see their societal evolution as glorious, but the price of human towns, of human cities, was nearly the death of fairykind. We survived, and we continue to plant trees and care for them. You continue to cut them down. *Do better.* You must. Start with Wimbledon Common. Plant trees until the forest's canopy stretches far and wide without end. Then keep planting. Everywhere.

Sage, the 12th sprite

Only ideas outnumber the books in **Hazel Ragaire**'s home. Breathing life into monster monstrosities and the just plain weird with a dash of horror or a sprinkle of sci-fi is kinda what she does. Enjoy recent works in several Ghost Orchid, Bag of Bones, and Dark Rose anthologies, and *Halloween Horror 3*. She loves discovering old forests' secrets. Find her at www.hazelragaire.com or Twitter @HRagaire.

The Amethyst Eye
by Blaise Langlois

It was dark on the path and the trees seemed to whisper to one another. Fairies and sprites darted among the shadows—or, at least, that's what Mimi Roche imagined. Each time she visited the park, she would toss a coin into the teapot fountain and wish that the stories her grandmother told her were true.

Today the path was empty, and Mimi couldn't have been happier. Lady Jane's Wood was her favourite part of Cannizaro Gardens, and she preferred to explore it without the hustle and bustle of other visitors. She breathed in the cool morning air and looked down at her feet. A pair of brown eyes looked back.

"Well, only if you promise not to tell Grandmama," she said, and she disconnected the small dog's lead from his collar. The brown and white Jack Russell Terrier replied with a quick bark, and his entire body wagged along with his tail. "Promise?" she asked. Mr Bones barked once more, and trotted ahead to sniff the flowers.

Mimi was admiring the rhododendrons and azaleas when she heard the sharp ring of a bicycle bell.

Brrring! Brrring!

Mr Bones froze midway across the path and Mimi cringed as a woman in an oversized feathered hat came barrelling toward him on a bicycle. "Look out!" Mimi cried. The woman narrowly missed the little dog, careering down the path without even looking back. *What a curious place to be riding a bicycle*, Mimi thought.

"Mr Bones," Mimi panted, as she caught up to the dog. "You have to be more careful. Now, sit," she commanded. Mr Bones sat, but his bum continued to wiggle in the dirt. "That's the last time I let you off lead," she scolded. "Grandmama trusts me to walk you while she's working. She'd kill me if anything happened to you."

Mimi reattached Mr Bones' lead, and they carried on

with their walk through the wood. There, just ahead, sitting on a bench, was the woman from earlier. She caught Mimi's eye and motioned for her to come over. The little girl pretended not to notice and was about to turn around when the woman called out, "Young lady. Don't I know your grandmother?"

I am in for it now, Mimi thought. Swallowing hard, she slowly shuffled over to the bench. Mr Bones barked, bearing his tiny, white teeth. "Quiet!" Mimi hissed, pulling back on his lead. "We're in enough trouble as it is."

"Your grandmother, Helene. She works at Cannizaro House, does she not?"

Mr Bones growled, and Mimi felt a flutter in her stomach. She wasn't supposed to talk to strangers, but if this woman knew her grandmother, she supposed it wouldn't hurt to be polite. "Yes, ma'am, she does." Looking down at her shoes, she blushed. "I am sorry my dog got in your way earlier."

The woman laughed, but her deep violet eyes did not.

"Really, it was my fault. I should watch where I am going," she said. "Let me make it up to you."

She reached into a large handbag and pulled out a white,

silk scarf. "I would love if you would accept this," she said. Mimi watched as the woman unwrapped the most beautiful necklace she had ever seen. A huge amethyst was set in the centre, and it seemed to wink at her like a giant eye.

"Oh, no. I couldn't."

"Nonsense," the woman said.

"No, really. I can't take it."

The woman's face grew dark, yet her eyes burned with a violet flame. "Don't you know it is rude to refuse a gift, girl? What *has* your grandmother been teaching you?" She reached her bony hand and grabbed Mimi's wrist.

Suddenly, Mr Bones—who had been pacing between Mimi and the stranger—leapt up and snatched the necklace. "Mr Bones! No!" Mimi shouted. The dog took off down the path, his lead dragging behind him. Mimi ran after him and was just about to snag his lead when he dived into the hedgerow.

Mimi dived through after him.

The pair burst through on the other side of the hedgerow, but Mimi didn't recognise this part of the park at all. The pale, pink sky seemed as though it were moving and the trees and shrubs glimmered in the strange light. *The sky isn't moving*, she thought. *Are those dragonflies?* Without warning, a swarm of them shot past her head, causing her to lose her balance. She toppled backwards and landed hard on her bottom. "Oof," she cried. Pushing herself up off the ground, Mimi felt something squishy under her hand. She turned it over and a red toadstool, or what was left of one anyway, stuck to her palm. One of the strange insects darted at her face. She swatted at it, but it continued to buzz at her.

"A fine mess you've made." It hovered in front of her face and pointed an accusatory finger. "Must be nice to be a giant and go around stomping on homes. Aren't you lucky the faire folk of these woods don't do that to you? For shame!" The sprite looked over its shoulder and, like lightning, sped away.

"What on earth are these things?" Mimi whispered. "And where are they going in such a hurry?" she asked, half expecting Mr Bones to answer.

Just then, thunder rumbled, and the sky darkened. The tiny creatures that had filled the sky were gone, leaving Mimi and Mr Bones alone. The hair on the back of Mimi's neck stood on end. *Hide*, she thought, and she quickly scooped up the dog and crouched behind the nearest shrub.

A huge shadow seemed to fall from the sky and Mimi shivered as a dragon with purple, shimmering scales landed with a *thud*. It unfurled its massive, black wings and beat them back and forth. Mimi was mesmerised.

"Psst. Over here," a voice called. A few feet away, Mimi could see a boy peeking from under a tree stump.

Mimi looked at the dragon, and once its back was turned, she made a quick dash to the boy's hiding place. Once inside, she found herself crouched next to a young boy with large, blue eyes and a crooked grin. He extended his hand. "The name's Theo. Theo Roberts."

Mimi set Mr Bones down and shook the boy's hand. "Mimi Roche. Where exactly are we?" she asked.

"Cannizaro Gardens," he replied causally. "Well, sort of. You're kind of between worlds." His wide grin showed a small gap between his front teeth. "Welcome to Middlegate."

"So, I'm in another dimension?"

"You could say that."

"What is that thing?" she asked, pointing to the creature outside.

"The Nether Dragon. It's been trying to escape from here

forever. Its mistress is trapped in the human world, but it cannot pass through without the amethyst eye," he said matter-of-factly.

Mimi thought for a moment. "Is that something like this?" she asked, revealing the pendant.

Theo's hand shot out and covered the necklace. "Are you crazy? That is some powerful, dark magic. Where did you get that?"

"A woman with violet eyes gave it to me."

Theo's eyes narrowed. "Casillia Crowe!" he said, spitting on the ground. "I knew she'd find a way to try to get back here."

"Who?"

"Pure evil, that's who. That fairy is responsible for wiping out half of Middlegate."

"So that's why she wanted me to have the necklace. Too bad for her, Mr Bones stole it." Mimi reached down to pet the dog, but he wasn't there. "Mr Bones!" she called softly. Prickles of cold sweat beaded on her forehead.

Theo flicked his eyes toward the clearing. "You mean him, right?"

How on earth did you get out there? Mimi thought.

Mr Bones and the Nether Dragon stood toe-to-toe and appeared to be arguing back and forth. The dog barked viciously as the dragon circled him. The huge beast leapt into the air and snatched Mr Bones up in its huge talons. Mimi made to bolt from their hiding spot, but Theo grabbed her arm.

"You can't go out there. Not yet. The dragon wants that amulet. It must sense the jewel is back in Middlegate. Otherwise, we wouldn't see it during the daytime. This is big trouble."

"Trouble or not, I am not leaving without my dog." Mimi said, shaking Theo free.

Theo lowered the hatch, and the space became dark. "Then this is the fastest way to get to him."

"Where are we going?"

"To the rose garden. It takes all of its victims there." Tears filled Mimi's eyes. Theo continued, "I mean—let's go save your dog!"

Theo whispered something into the darkness, and the walls began to glow. Tiny bioluminescent plants lined the walls. "Follow me," he said.

They quickly reached the end of the tunnel, and Theo

lead the way up a small ladder. He cracked open the trapdoor and peeked out. Mimi squeezed in beside him.

Mr Bones was sitting in the centre of the garden. Alone. Mimi called him, but he seemed unable to move. Seizing the moment, she pushed open the hatch and ran to him. "No, Mimi! It's a trap!" shouted Theo.

The dragon seemed to materialise from thin air as it swooped down, striking at her with its claws. She did a front roll, avoiding its talons as they tore up the earth beside her. The beast blew a stream of hot blue flame, but Mimi managed to dodge it and ducked behind a large section of rose bush. The heat was intense, and she turned her face away as the Nether Dragon decimated the bush with its flame.

Mimi was trapped.

"The amulet!" Theo screamed. Mimi grasped the jewel at her throat and found it warm to the touch. Suddenly, strange, new words were streaming from Mimi's mouth. She kept chanting, and the dragon screeched in pain. Violet flames rose into the air as its body burst into smoke, which rushed toward the amulet. As if plucked from her hand, the pendant rose into the air, and the Nether Dragon was sucked into the gemstone in a puff of smoke.

The amulet settled on Mimi's chest. The dog, now free from the dragon's spell, ran over, jumping on Mimi.

She scratched his head and looked at Theo. "How do we get home?"

"First, there's someone I'd like you to meet."

Mimi and Mr Bones—lead on this time—followed Theo from one garden into another. They came upon a beautiful statue of a woman and a fawn. The woman in the statue lifted her head."

"She's a friend," Theo said.

He and the woman spoke in a language Mimi didn't understand, but one she felt oddly comfortable with. The woman turned to Mimi and smiled.

"Child, you used some very old magic today," she said. Mimi blushed. "However, the power that amulet wields is not one meant for the human world, or for human hands. Casillia cannot enter our world—especially now that we have the amulet, and her dragon is imprisoned. We are safe. The amulet must be given to the council. And now, my dear, it is time for you to head home."

🦔 🦔 🦔

Mimi stepped out of the fountain and Mr Bones followed. He shook off the water and barked joyously.

"My petite rose," a voice called out.

"Grandmama!" said Mimi, running over and wrapping her arms around her grandmother.

"Why are you so late?" she asked. Mr Bones gave three sharp barks. "Well, is that so?" Grandmama said. She held Mimi close as a blackbird flew overhead. "The bus will be along soon. Let's go home. It is about time I explained a few things to you."

Mimi smiled. "Yes, Grandmama. Home sounds perfect."

Emerging author, **Blaise Langlois**, will never turn down the chance to tell a creepy story. You are sure to find her writing in between teaching and raising four beautiful children, or feverishly scratching out ideas (which to the chagrin of her supportive husband, usually occurs just after midnight). She has a penchant for horror, sci-fi, and fantasy. Her publications include short fiction and poetry through Eerie River Publishing, Pulp Factory E-zine, Black Hare Press, Space and Time Magazine, Black Spot Books and Ghost Orchid Press. You can learn more about her writing journey by visiting her blog at: www.ravenfictionca.wordpress.com.

Lucy's Rabbits
by Megan Feehley

Little Lucy loved the rabbits
hopping in the weeds.

They jumped to her and sniffed her shoes
before she gave them seeds.

Soft and plump, with big black eyes,
they wiggled in her arms.

The way they napped upon her lap—
she must've had a charm.

Those bunnies loved seeing Little Lucy in the field.

As when that hungry wolf came down—

She was a splendid shield.

Megan Feehley is an emerging author from San Diego, California. She has a deep fascination for the weird and chaotic, and spends much of her free time reading psychological horror and thriller novels. The less sleep it gives her, the better.

Grace's Kingdom
by Leanbh Pearson

race felt the anxiety build as she walked towards the school gates, her mother watching from the sidewalk, offering a wave of encouragement. But Grace knew from experience that all the rules her mother upheld disappeared the moment she crossed that indivisible barrier between the Real World and School. Despite the concerted efforts from her parents, the meetings between them and her schoolteachers, and then later the school principal, nothing had ever changed. The only constant Grace knew was the bullying taunts from her 'peers,' and the constant reminder of how different she was from them. Already, she could hear their shouted cruelties, words that stung far worse than unkind pinches or shoves.

"Freak!" someone called out to her, the shrill laughter that always accompanied such witticisms swiftly following.

"Where's your friends, loser?" Another remark that cut deeply and met with uproarious laughter from the other children.

Grace bit her bottom lip, blinking back the welling tears from her eyes. Immediately, she veered from the path, sprinting into the dense undergrowth and tangled vines that filled the space beside the playground fence. Beyond the school fences was the open expanse of Wimbledon Common. Here, the others would never dare follow her. Here, she would find Grace's Kingdom, where only she was welcome.

Her eyes were closed, allowing the dappled light to calm her. Then, when she was ready, Grace opened her eyes to the wonder that was her Kingdom. The forest floor was mossy, but not in the sense of the moist, earthy vegetation of the Real World. Here in Grace's Kingdom, the moss was velvety and, running her fingers through it like an animal's fur, the moss reacted to her touch. She smiled as the pastel-coloured spheres lifted from the forest floor, dispersing into the air in sherbet-tasting mist.

Grace got to her feet, the tingle of sherbet still on her tongue. Walking across the mossy carpet, she smiled as more confectionery clouds puffed into the atmosphere around her. Peering at the ground, she saw small mushrooms that released sugar-sweet bubbles as she passed, reminding her of the yearly event she had watched on television, when underwater coral spawned to begin new generations.

Above her, a strange bird called, its voice more musical than a lark, and sweeter than a nightingale. Squinting up into the trees, Grace noticed the curling vines were impossible creations too, the multi-hued greens twisted into long vines of liquorice. She saw the bird then, its jewel-coloured plumage and fiery eye. It turned its majestic head to regard her, called once more before taking to wing, the bright fiery trail of its tail shimmering through the forest. Grace gasped in surprise, watching the creature disappear into the twilit sky.

Night was falling fast. Grace frowned, unsure how much

time she had spent walking along the mossy forest floor.

"Lady Grace?" a tiny voice called, piping, but familiar.

"Hello?" she asked, half-turning to regard a diminutive being standing atop one of the mushrooms.

"It is our pleasure to welcome you again, Lady."

"Have I met you before?"

"Not me, but one of my kin. Dandelion, at your service, Lady."

The little figure effected a flourishing bow, the white dandelion-fluff of his hair (for which he was clearly named) wafting in the breeze. His face was pale, cheeks ruddy with good health, his body stout but movement fluid. Grace studied his clothing; the pastel colours of his overalls seemed woven of fairy floss. She thought about the sugary scent that filled the air and considered it likely that Dandelion and his kin all wore clothing woven from the fibres of this land. Most of what Grace had observed occurring naturally here was formed from fantastic confectionary.

"Shall we return you to your world now, Lady?"

Grace startled as Dandelion's piping voice broke into her thoughts. "Yes," she agreed distractedly, thinking of the world she had left behind. "But I don't really want to."

"Be brave, Lady," her small companion rallied. "You are always welcome here; this is your Kingdom, after all. But you cannot stay forever."

"Why not?" She asked sulkily.

"My kin are guardians to this land, Lady. We are exactly as you see us; beings of purest confection, dreamscapes, and fantasies. You are our honoured guest here, but you must always return to your world lest it forgets you."

Grace bit her bottom lip, unwilling to leave, but feeling the steady flow of the Real World flooding into her Kingdom. Sighing, she relinquished herself to the tide, allowing Dandelion to dissipate in the breeze as though he were blown away like one of the sherbet clouds.

👑 👑 👑

Grace sat in the dense tangle of vines where she had hidden earlier. The vines were no longer twining green liquorice, the mushrooms at her feet did not emit sherbet clouds, and Dandelion was nowhere to be seen. Grace straightened, and squaring her shoulders, recalling Dandelion's rallying challenge against her fears. Aware she could return to the Kingdom whenever she needed it, Grace strode into the light of the playground, prepared to face whatever combatants might stand against her.

Leanbh Pearson lives on Ngunnawal Country, in Canberra, Australia. An LGBTQI dark fiction author inspired by mythology, folklore, archaeology, history, and the environment, her short fiction features in numerous anthologies. Partially fictional, she is a keen nature and wildlife photographer, bookshop, and Museum devotee, and enjoys the Australian wilderness with her dogs (the canine assistants). Leanbh's alter-ego is an academic in archaeology and prehistory. Follow her at www.leanbhpearson.com, and on Twitter, Facebook, and Instagram @leanbhpearson.

Dragon Breath
by Maggie D. Grace

eorge had gorged himself on the picnic feast, then lain down near the fragrant heather dozing. He awoke to a persistent nudge on his foot. Rubbing his eyes and peering down, he saw the weirdest creature he'd ever seen. He swore it looked just like a tiny dragon, but he knew that couldn't be true. He rubbed his eyes again and sat up. Thinking it was perhaps some new species of lizard, he slowly reached down, trying to capture it. Just as he attempted to scoop it up, a spark of fire shot out of its nose. George recoiled as he peered at his singed knuckles. More scared than hurt, he jumped up and jammed his injured fingers into his mouth.

The lizardy creature sat upright, winked at George, and scuttled up his pant leg. In a flash, he was atop George's shoulder. Too alarmed to move, he stood transfixed. A tiny tongue flicked out of the lizard's mouth, tickling George's ear.

A strangely sibilant voice whispered, "We don't cotton to you lot round here. Why don't you take your big feet and go home?" Taking another lick of his ear, the creature scurried back down George, then disappeared into thin air.

Dumbfounded, George searched around the greenery looking for the odd dragon, if that's what it actually was. Before long, his mum called him to go home. He thought about telling her about his strange encounter, but decided to keep it to himself for a while. After all, who would believe he had met an actual dragon? He looked down at his slightly scorched knuckles and giggled to himself. Next time he visited Wimbledon Common, he'd be sure to pack a net.

Maggie D. Brace, a life-long denizen of Maryland, teacher, gardener, basketball player and author attended St. Mary's College, where she met her soulmate, and Loyola University, Maryland. She has written *'Tis Himself: The Tale of Finn MacCool* and *Grammy's Glasses,* and has multiple short works and poems in various anthologies. She remains a humble scrivener and avid reader. @MaggieDBrace

Living Confections
by Rachel Ginsburg

Maxine went down the creaky wooden stairs, her small hand gripping the thick walnut banister. Being a fairy, she had wings, but they felt stiff and broken from lack of use, like an umbrella discarded after a storm. She hadn't flown since her parents died a year ago, as fairies never fly while in mourning. Her Uncle Rupert (who had taken her in) told her it was time to move on. She was being ridiculous, and he should know, he said, being a fairy elder.

Maxine opened the secret door behind a hinged mirror that connected the living room to Uncle Rupert's steel experimentation tube. The dense foliage outside hid the structure from trespassers, while the inside of the tube held the beginning stages of Rupert's life's work. The tube contained hundreds of his Living Confection prototypes: crawling glow-in-the-dark worms that tasted like sugar topped mulberries and blooming phosphorescent flowers that had lemongrass and pomegranate notes upon the tongue.

"Uncle Rupert, I'm here!" Maxine called out, and then heard her uncle climbing the stairs that connected to his basement kitchen laboratory. Rupert peeked out from behind the door with his moon face and orange hard hat in silhouette.

"I see you've finally got out of bed. Since you're here, you can help. Shield your eyes," he said, and he turned on the floodlights that made the edible glowworms and flowers shrink back in intimidation. Maxine closed her eyes against the onslaught of high beams.

"Now open them!"

Out flew hundreds of butterflies in a dazzling translucent cloud. The tiny, winged creatures landed on the flower petals, the humps of the glowworms and skidded across the stainless walls of the tube, getting used to their new wings.

A tinge of jealousy shot up through Maxine, as she had not flown with such ease in so long.

Uncle Rupert begged Maxine to stick out her tongue to catch one in her mouth.

"Please, Maxine, for me?" His hands came together like a praying mantis. She wondered what she had got herself into.

One flew past Maxine's cheek because her teeth formed an unintentional protective cage. Then she got up her strength—from her toes on up through her nose, as her mum taught her—and opened her mouth and caught one. It was crunchy and delicate, like glass made from spun sugar. Its sweetness tasted like nature on a dewy, sunlit morning. Since she lost her parents, she hadn't experienced anything that lovely.

"What do you think?" asked Rupert.

"Can I have another?"

"You can have another if you do me a big favour."

That sounded bad. "What is it, Uncle Rupert?"

"The only way I can make my living confections is with this superpowered, highly illegal dust."

"Wait. There is more than one kind of dust?" Maxine

mimed her head exploding.

"Maxine, this is pixie dust, not fairy. Our dust does so little," he sighed.

"Flying's a good one," Maxine said.

"True, but pretty mundane." Rupert sat so close to Maxine she could smell his decaying teeth from all his samplings of sugar. "Last week, the pixie elders found out what I was buying and banished me from Wimbledon Common, and now I'm out of dust. But you can sneak in and meet with Ponder, my pixie dust supplier. The guards won't be tracking you and your young gardenia scent. You see, they have my dank old fairy smell on file. I'm going to make a deal with you. If you procure an ounce of pixie dust, I will bring your mum back to life with the leftovers. It will be a sweet, edible version of your mum, but close enough!"

"Really? Can you bring back my dad, too?"

"Now, don't be greedy. One parent at a time." Although she was disappointed Rupert couldn't bring both parents back, Maxine hugged her uncle, knocking his hard hat to the ground. Rupert wasn't used to being touched and backed away. Maxine couldn't wait to be in the arms of her beloved mother again.

Uncle Rupert gave Maxine directions to find Ponder. As a fairy who lived on Putney Heath, she had never been to Wimbledon Common where the pixies lived. She heard it might be filled with wild animals twice her size. Finding strength from her toes, up through her nose, she took her satchel and went.

Rupert's map was clear, drawn carefully on honey brickle paper, edible parchment he invented years ago. She walked carefully past upright blades of grass, blue cornflowers and bright red ladybugs minding their own business, weaving in and out of stalks and stems. All the while, she was on the lookout for large animals that could eat her.

She was feeling a little funny in her tummy, but she was used to that after her parents died in a tragic accident. They were baking for the Fairy Queen when they met their demise; her parents got burnt to a crisp by trying to save the royal china service during a kitchen fire. They were put into a double coffin and Maxine had to identify their bodies: the charcoal lift of their cheekbones, the swoop of their ashen hair, the muddled mix of their singed wings, and their sparkling clothing gone drab.

Soon after, Maxine went to live with her Uncle Rupert, who was on a mission to create living edible versions of every creature on earth. Not just inert candy replicas motionless in a shop's glass display case, actual breathing, moving, sweet renditions of all living things. Her mother, while she was alive, would call him "Crazy Uncle Rupert" or "my daft brother" not realising her daughter would be reared by him soon enough.

High on a toadstool, Maxine saw Ponder just beyond the purple rhododendron patch. Maxine had never met a pixie before; they were supposed to be quite mean and nasty. From a distance, Ponder reminded her of a grasshopper in his lime green suit. He was not as intimidating as she thought. He was practising a sort of tai chi on the curve of the towering fungi.

"Excuse me, you must be Ponder."

"Hush, lass, be very quiet. We wouldn't want you to be banned, too! What have you brought me?"

"That's rude," Maxine said with her hands on her hips, looking up at him, "You can't ask me what I brought before inviting me in. It's like opening a present without looking at the card."

"Your uncle told me you were a smartass," Ponder said and then changed his tone to pure treacle. "Greetings, my lass. Come inside."

He fluttered down from the top of the mushroom, did an air somersault mid-flight, then opened a small door and invited Maxine in. Since a pixie is even smaller than a fairy, Maxine had to duck to go inside his spotted home.

"Nettle tea?"

"Let's cut to the chase. You know why I'm here."

Inside Ponder's tiny, neat home, Maxine gave him three edible butterflies fluttering around in a jar.

"Only three?" Ponder asked.

"That's what my uncle gave me."

"I could have sworn Rupert said four. One for me and three for the dust guards I must pay off. I think you ate one, lass. Be honest. A little snack along the way?"

"No sir. But I'll be back. I'll bring you more next time."

"I'll be waiting for my next delivery from you, lass. Let me get Rupert's package." Ponder spun around on his heel, reached inside a hollow in the wall, and gave Maxine a bag that seemed to glow from within. "Be careful with this. Give it straight to Rupert."

Maxine headed home, licking the sugary remnant of the missing butterfly's wings from her lips. She brought her uncle enough dust to make thousands of living confections and bring her mum back to life.

৬৬ ৬৬ ৬৬

A week went by. There was still no Mum.

"What about Mum and our deal?" Maxine yelled as she ran down the stairs, making extra loud thumps.

"Calm down, child. What about your mum?"

"Uh, bringing her back? Making her live again? The dust? Remember your promise after I risked life and limb to visit Ponder?"

"Don't worry, I'll bring her back someday. But first I have to perfect less complex creatures. You saw what happened to my misfits that I had to melt back down to sugar. Tragic, indeed. A human is incredibly complex, takes 1,000 granules of dust. Currently, I'm making a monkey that tastes like hot chocolate. Your mum can wait."

Maxine stomped upstairs to her bedroom and slammed her door. If Rupert wasn't going to do it, she would bring

Mum back herself.

She began secretly to visit Ponder, bringing him living confections she stole from Rupert in exchange for more dust. Meanwhile, she kept notes on what Rupert was doing down in the basement. She took his recipe book and memorised the formulas. Maxine practised making her own living bugs, flowers, and rodents in the lab while Rupert was asleep. She was perfecting her skills so much that Rupert praised her for being such a surprisingly good apprentice. She still had hope that Rupert would follow through on his promise to bring back Mum, but the more time went by, the more her hope vanished.

♔ ♔ ♔

One day, Maxine heard singing and dancing coming from Rupert's basement kitchen lab. She saw through a crack in the floorboards that he had used the dust to create a living, breathing flour and sugar version of himself.

"How dare he make a twin of himself before bringing back Mum," Maxine thought. "I'll make him pay for this!"

She stealthily followed Rupert as he pranced down the pebbled path to the palace, high-fiving and elbow-bumping his edible twin, seeming already to celebrate his eventual success. Rupert had spoken of opening a living confection shop on the palace esplanade. Maxine imagined he was going to propose this to the Queen when he showed off his twin.

Leaping their way toward the palace, the sun further baked Rupert's sugary alter-ego, causing wafts of the man-shaped patisserie to fill the air. Maxine heard the Queen's regular-sized watch-cats' meow with hunger, so she climbed a sycamore to wait for the duo to pass below. She reached into her satchel and sprinkled sugar on Rupert's head. The watch-cats' noses caught wind of the lovely smells. Their thin-lipped mouths—with sharp teeth—watered, and they pounced on the two frolicking men, eating Rupert and his sugary twin for lunch. Maxine was frozen as she watched the cats gobble down her uncle, first head, then torso, then feet. After the shock wore off, she was quite pleased with herself.

Maxine had to work quickly to leave the Heath. The Queen sent out a proclamation to capture Rupert's murderer, since the guards found his sugared hair along the path one of the watch-cats spat out like a hairball. Fortunately, Maxine had enough pixie dust to make her mum return. With a smidge of DNA from her mum's hair that she found in her brush, a few kilos of flour, sugar and butter and Rupert's proprietary rubber plant elixir, she was able to bake a singular, beautiful, sugary mum, wings and all. She was heartbroken that she didn't have enough dust to make her dad return and planned to sneak a visit to Ponder as soon as possible.

As Mum came out of the oven, she sat up on the rack and stretched as if she had just woken from slumber. Her favourite frock baked right onto her with its fondant frills. As Mum was getting used to her limbs and wings, Maxine tested hers out as well. She didn't know where they were going, but her wings felt so good finally stretched out after all that time spent folded and dormant. They escaped just as they heard the ferociously meowing watch-cats getting closer. Maxine had worried her salty tears would melt Mum, but they only added more shimmer.

Rachel Ginsburg is a psychotherapist in private practice and writes fiction as often as she can. Her short stories have been featured in the *Gluttony* anthology from Black Hare Press, *Tigershark,* and *Hags on Fire.* She is currently working on a novel.

No Fairyland
by Tracy Davidson

There's something living in the trees,
It calls to children on the breeze.

With whispers buzzing in their head,
They move in closer, feeling no dread.

Until... oh no, the creature strikes!
Putting children's heads upon park spikes.

It feeds on bones, blood, and bellies,
Turning all to jams and jellies.

So, on the Common, please beware

Of zombie fairies lurking there.

Tracy Davidson lives in Warwickshire, England, and writes poetry and flash fiction. Her work has appeared in various publications and anthologies, including: *Poet's Market, Mslexia, Atlas Poetica, Modern Haiku, The Binnacle, A Hundred Gourds, Shooter, Journey to Crone, The Great Gatsby* anthology, *WAR, In Protest: 150 Poems for Human Rights.*

Poster Children
by L.N. Hunter

When the bars and restaurants of the village of Wimbledon close in the wee hours of the morning and the streets finally empty, the people in the shop window ads can relax and make their presence known. Among the war-painted and angry-looking wrestlers in the poster for next week's bouts, Jeremy is the first to break the silence. "Thank goodneth for that, my jaw wath cramping with all that grimathing—why do I alwayth have to be the one who lookth like he'th gurning?"

Bruno doesn't respond. He's trying to peer around the corner to catch more than just a glimpse of Serious Jane and Party Jane in the High Street optician's two-for-one stylish frames ad. "Hubba hubba, girlies, get yourselves over here and say hello to a real man."

James, in the optician's window across the road, wearing plain glass lenses—his eyesight's perfect, but a job's a job—in Gucci frames and tasteful cardigan, sniffs and turns away. Serious Jane always tells him to ignore the wrestlers. "There's more to life than Neanderthal-browed morons like Bruno," she says.

James does quite like the Jane twins. He finds Party's purple hair, pink horn-rimmed glasses, and extroverted manner a bit intimidating. And Serious, in her more sober wire frames and lab coat, always seems to have her head in a book. He sighs. If only there were a Jane halfway between them.

The Janes normally enjoy each other's company, which is just as well since they're stuck side-by-side day after day. However, Party Jane has a headache tonight and tries to persuade Serious Jane to swap places. All she really wants is a little bit of peace and quiet, instead of going clubbing with the guys in the wrestling ad. "Look, I'll even let you wear my spangly top—the one you've been coveting since these new posters went up."

Just then, a wail comes from across the street: "Look what they've done to me!" There's a synchronised gasp as all eyes turn towards Supermarket Sue in the Tesco's near the station. She's sporting a bushy moustache and ugly thick-rimmed black spectacles, thanks to the evening's graffiti artists.

Beekeeper Bill, sharing the same window, wraps a fatherly arm around her shoulders and says, "There, there."

Much tutting ensues, and a crude stick figure, also in thick black paint, on the wall beside Sue's poster says, "I'm really sorry about what's happened to you, Sue, but don't worry, it'll wash off in the next rain. I know, because that's when I usually vanish. Those louts come round here every evening, but they're getting no better at painting. Banksy needn't have any worries about their competition—I'm the best they've ever managed to paint. They'll be back tomorrow, and we really ought to do something about them before things get worse."

James clears his throat. "Excuse me, everybody. I've got a suggestion. What if we douse the streetlights around here early tomorrow? That'll make the rest of the public leave this bit of the village early, and we can set a trap for the yobs.

Here's what we'll do…"

The next night, the poster people are ready. The street is dark, only the moon and shop security lights illuminating the scene. Two teenage boys dressed in heavy metal tee-shirts and tatty jeans approach. The taller one, additionally sporting a scuffed leather jacket, is carrying a can of spray paint, and he tells the other boy to keep a lookout while he gets to work. He approaches the wrestlers and mumbles something to his companion about giving them afros and beards.

With a hissing sound, a waist-high mist suddenly envelops them.

Party Jane had switched on the fog generator in her poster background's nightclub and is directing the flow out on to the street. Serious Jane aims lasers from her poster's lab at the nightclub's disco balls, scattering brightly coloured spots of light across the fog and up and down the walls. Serious Jane is playing spooky music on the piano. Party joins in, screeching her fingernails down the window while making howling wolf noises.

As the boys jump round in surprise, Bruno leans out of the poster and growls, "We don't like your sort around here.

You're going to pay for what you've done."

Stickman shrieks a maniacal laugh, and the boys pale.

Beekeeper Bill opens his honey pots, and with a cry of, "Fly, moi lovelies," shakes loose a swarm of bees. He thrusts a finger in the direction of the boys, and shouts, "Attaaaack!"

Making tearing noises, the bees rip themselves from the supermarket poster and buzz directly towards the youths.

The boys scream and drop their paint. They whirl in panic and run, but by now, the mist is above their heads, and they can't even see each other, let alone where they're going. Every turn they make, they're confronted by a leering face or the roar of angry bees. Tripping over kerbstones and bouncing off trees, they make it as far as the common before they slam into each other and knock themselves unconscious.

Early next morning, a pair of patrolling police constables find the boys lying where they fell. Both boys sport black painted moustaches and glasses, and the taller one has something rude drawn on his forehead as well. The police officers prod the youths with the toes of their boots to wake them.

The boys sit up and clutch at the officers' legs, spouting

some harebrained story about a mysterious fog and ghost people coming to life. They collapse, sobbing, "Help us, please. The bees. The bees!"

PC Jones mutters something about morons spending too much time sniffing the contents of their spray cans and deserving all the unpleasant hallucinations they get. PC Atkinson nods in agreement, but is only half paying attention. She's wondering about the detailed drawings of bees someone seems to have carefully cut out and scattered on the grass around the boys.

L.N. Hunter's publications include *The Feather and the Lamp,* a comic fantasy novel, and short stories in anthologies *War* and *Trickster's Treats 3,* among others. There have also been papers in the IEEE *Transactions on Neural Networks,* which are probably somewhat less relevant and definitely less fun. When not writing, L.N. unwinds in a disorganised home in rural Cambridgeshire, UK, along with two cats and a soulmate. Find out more or get in touch via @L.N.Hunter.writer on Facebook.

The Wimbledon Wyvern
by D.J. Tyrer

One day on Wimbledon Common
Dog walkers and strollers express surprise
At the new bulge in the ground

Nascent hill, earth cracking

Sudden soil explosion

Something soars skyward

Wyvern takes flight

Unseen for centuries

Dragon head and bat-like wings

Snaps up a few people

Then, flies away, westward

Presumably seeking a place to nest

The Wimbledon Wyvern will wait in Wales

For its hungry brood to hatch…

D.J. Tyrer is the person behind Atlantean Publishing, and has been published in The Rhysling Anthology 2016, and issues of Cyaegha, Enchanted Conversation, The Horrorzine, Illumen, Scifaikuest, Sirens Call, Spectral Realms, and Star*Line. SuperTrump and A Wuhan Whodunnit are available to download from the Atlantean Publishing website.

Ms Sundew
by Laura Nettles

The wooden stairs creaked on the porch at the dark red painted house in Wimbledon Common. Red like the hair of the woman who lived there, all alone. She wasn't going to be alone for long.

Creak. Creak. Twelve-year-old Jimmy's heart pounded in his ears as he climbed the rickety steps. His brown hair was stuck up from sweat. Ever since his little sister, Carey, had gone missing yesterday, like the black cat she had gone out looking for, he couldn't shake off the feeling that he was next.

He moved the torch to see between the steps and under the house. His blood froze. There was one of Carey's yellow shoes—the ones she had been wearing while running around with missing cat posters. She had been here at the maroon house across the street.

Shuffling footsteps echoed in the house, coming closer. Jimmy jumped the last step up to the porch and crawled under a bench sagging with the weight of many potted plants displayed on its splintering surface. The door opened and a pair of bare feet covered in dirt stopped next to his nose.

"Hello, my pretties. How are you this fine night?"

Was she talking to him? No. The plants. Weird.

"Don't worry, Lilith, Ambrosia will recover from that evil cat messing with her. We will have some extra fine fertiliser soon. You'll all grow so big, you'll need to be transferred to the backyard!" Her hands brushed against the rustling green, yellow, and purple leaves. Then, a cracking sound, as if bark was torn from a tree, filled the cool night air.

A deep watery voice, which seemed to be coming from Ms Sundew, started to sing in a language Jimmy had never heard. As the dancing words rang through Jimmy's ears, he saw the vines of the plants grow longer, sprouting new leaves. A quiet squelching sound, and her voice returned to

normal.

"Good night, my darlings. Sleep well."

The dirty feet went back into the house.

Jimmy's chest hurt from not breathing for so long. He took deep breaths of air that smelled like dirt after rain. That creepy lady had his sister. He had to rescue her!

Carefully, he crawled out from under the plants. Their spindly vines felt like they were clinging to his shirt, scratching his arms, trying to pull him back towards them. He shook them off and crept towards the door.

There was no light on in the house. It was dark like a cave since the curtains were drawn. Was she keeping more secrets besides his sister in there?

The door handle was cold and sticky, smelling like honey. It swung open without a sound.

Light from the torch shone down the front hall, illuminating wooden flooring. As he turned the beam of light, he saw someone his height. In terror, he jumped a few steps back, until he realised it was just a mirror. He breathed a sigh of relief.

Down the hall he went. The kitchen on the right was completely empty. No plates, cups, or food to be seen. The living room was full of large potted plants, while framed pictures of nature hung on the wall. Yellow strips of flypaper hung from the ceiling, coated in twitching insects. The curtains moved slightly in the night breeze.

If he were a scary person, where would he hide his sister? His heart sank—the basement, of course.

Since this house had the same layout as his family's house, he knew the way to get there. Past the bedrooms and down the stairs.

He tiptoed down the long, dark hallway, past rooms with doors cracked open. The bathroom tub was filled with lily pads, their closed white flowers poking up over the side, reflecting his light like pale skulls. One of the bedrooms had a large snake plant tucked in bed, tall, spiky leaves stabbing into the fluffed pillow.

Jimmy's hands were sweating. Why was this lady so obsessed with plants? The last bedroom had the door closed. Ms Sundew must be in there. Just in case, he dropped to the floor and crawled past. Better to be safe.

At last, he was at the basement door. It was large, warped, and mouldy, as if it were usually wet. It didn't hang straight anymore.

Pushing it open, Jimmy crept down the stairs one at a time, too scared to call out for Carey. He didn't have to.

Meow. Mr Hissy? Quickly slipping down the rest of the ten steps, Jimmy swung his torch around and froze. There were roots covering the dirt walls of the unfinished basement. Big thick ones, and long thin ones. And held hostage in the middle of them all was Carey, clutching the black cat, Mr Hissy. Carey's blonde curls were dirty and tangled, her blue dress slightly torn.

"Jimmy!" she cried.

"Shh!" Jimmy breathed. "I'm coming, just hang on."

"There are pruning shears on the bench. I can't reach them, but they should help," Carey whispered.

"On it." He ran to the workstation filled with empty pots and found a polished pair of very sharp clippers. Turning, he slotted them around the first root holding Carey in place.

Snip. Scream. A loud bang of a door bouncing off a wall echoed from upstairs as the inhuman screaming continued. It sounded like something gargling wet glass marbles, shrieking as they rubbed against each other.

Bam! The basement door flew open, hitting the dirt wall so hard some chunks of soil fell onto the stairs.

Jimmy and Carey screamed.

Ms Sundew's face and wig were peeled like bark ribbons down to her chest, revealing a mass of large sticky leaves and a huge pod that was her dark green skull. Red wet hairs stuck out from the leaves in all directions, reflecting the glow of the torch. The large pod split down the middle from top to bottom, a giant mouth with teeth dripping goo.

Quickly, Jimmy cut the last roots holding Carey in place. With each cut, Ms Sundew made a garbled cry. By the time she reached the bottom of the stairs, Mr Hissy had dashed out of Carey's arms and made for the door at the top.

A long green arm with sticky red hairs came out of Ms Sundew's back, reaching for the cat. With a hiss, Mr Hissy dodged her curling, grasping arm and sprinted out of the door. He was safe.

But Jimmy and Carey were not.

"Split up and run around her," Jimmy whispered to his sister. "I'll go left, you go right."

With a nod, Carey raced around the approaching Ms Sundew.

"You won't eat my sister!" yelled Jimmy as he ran left, bearing the pruning shears and torch.

His distraction worked. The dark, sticky head of the plant woman turned to him, vine arms stretching out toward his hands.

Raising the shears, he cut at the appendages, but they pulled back just in time.

"Get out, Carey!" he yelled. She had stopped at the top of the stairs, frozen.

Trembling, she dashed out the mouldy door with her one yellow shoe.

Jimmy backed up the stairs, holding the clippers out in front of him in case Ms Sundew tried to attack again.

Three steps to go. Two steps to go. The roots sprang from the wall, tangling around the pruning shears, yanking them from his grip.

In terror, Jimmy spun and ran the rest of the way, feeling vines grabbing at his ankles and hair.

He dared not look back.

Past the bedrooms, where the snake plant was now sitting up in bed. Past the living room where the potted plants were moving like a fierce wind was whipping around. Out of the silent door and down the creaky steps. He grabbed Carey's hand, and together they sprinted for home.

They never went back for her other shoe.

Laura Nettles is a California girl living in Canada. She lights creatures for horror films by day, and pens terror by night. Follow her journey and read some of her fiction at lauranettles.com.

Don't Linger
on the Shore
by Gabby Gilliam

On the Common down in Wimbledon
   where windmill scratches sky,
   you might find the unexpected
out of the corner of your eye.

She creeps beneath the duckweed
stalking her young prey,
those foolish unwary children
perched at the water's edge to play.

Her skin as green as the algae

that grow between her sharpened teeth,

she'll snatch them from the soggy reeds

and drag them down into the deep

where mother's cries will never find them

where the sunlight cannot reach

where there is only the dark and the iron grasp

of the bog hag Jenny Greenteeth.

Gabby Gilliam lives in the DC metro area. Her poetry has appeared most recently in *Bluing the Blade, Cauldron Anthology,* and the *Medusa Rises* anthology from Mythos Poets Society. She can be found online at gabbygilliam.squarespace.com.

When Curiosity
Saved the Cat
by Henry Herz

As a wee lass, I gained a keen love for animals. Perhaps it was because my father worked as a veterinarian, or maybe it was from Grandfather's whimsical tales of legendary beasts. Most likely, though, it was because we lived a stone's throw from Wimbledon Common. Speaking of stone's throw, I eventually developed a decidedly unladylike (according to Grandmum) throwing arm from skipping flat stones across the surface of Rushmere Pond.

By the age of twelve, I knew the southern half of the

Common as well as any park ranger. I learned about the reserve's wildlife and could tell a common shrew from a pygmy shrew and a bank vole from a field vole. No doubt, had I told her, Grandmum would've held a dim view of that skill as well.

Recently, my explorations took a most unwelcome turn. With each visit, I found a slaughtered animal, mostly rabbits and weasels. Tears ran down my cheeks. The grass around each animal's roughly severed head was stained dark red. Storms of flies buzzed. To this day, that sound makes me nauseous. Something was wrong. One day, after discovering a dead fox, I trudged home, my throat tight.

After dinner, I threw on a flannel jacket and grabbed a torch. I told my parents I was going to visit my friend Dee. When they smiled and told me to be home by 8 PM, my gut twisted with guilt.

I entered the Common. Darkness fell, but the moon had not yet risen. I paused and closed my eyes to listen to nature's lullaby: branches rustling in the gentle breeze, the croaking of frogs, cricket-song. A sudden gust rushed over me, raising the hairs on the back of my neck, though I wasn't cold. I swept my torch beam in a circle. Nothing.

I strode past Bluegate Pond. Deep in the woods, the hair on my arms stiffened. I hadn't noticed until then, but the night had wrapped me in a blanket of silence. The crickets and frogs no longer sang. Even the breeze had taken leave.

Dead leaves rustled along the ground. *Without a breeze?* I wondered. I crouched behind a tree and froze. Mice, rabbits, and a squirrel skittered by, paying no attention to me in their single-minded urge to flee. I shivered. Following an impulse, I shut off my torch and held my breath.

A thunderous roar preceded fierce snarls. The latter cut off suddenly. I felt a strong urge to run, but dared not make a sound. Shivering uncontrollably, I peeked around the tree trunk.

Maybe forty metres away, a muscular catlike creature hunched over a poor badger lying motionless on the grass. Red fur covered the monster's huge body, four legs, and a tail that writhed like a snake. A bushy mane framed its face, and an impressive rack of antlers crowned its enormous head.

My stomach knotted as the monster effortlessly severed the badger's thick neck with a quick snap of powerful jaws.

Gore dripped from long fangs. Eyes glowed a sickly

yellow. The monster twisted its neck to gnaw on the badger's body, revealing a shiny metallic box with wires and red flashing lights, somehow attached to the top of its head.

I blinked to clear the nightmarish vision. No luck. My mouth fell open in realisation. This odd combination of lion and deer could be the Stratford Lyon from my grandfather's tales, though he had never mentioned a box mechanism. Despite the utter strangeness of the creature, the metal struck me as most out of place.

Disgusting sounds of flesh tearing echoed in my brain. I had planned to scare off an animal by throwing stones, but what could I do against the Stratford Lyon? My pulse raced. *Time to leave.*

Slow and quiet, I told myself, despite the overwhelming urge to sprint. I crept toward home as the monster gorged. Until I stepped on a dry twig. That crackle sound will haunt me for the rest of my days.

The Lyon's head snapped up. Its haunting yellow eyes locked on mine. It roared.

Throwing stealth to the wind, I sprinted for home between sturdy trunks.

The beast bounded after me. Luckily, its rack of antlers

was so broad that the Lyon couldn't directly pursue me through the thickly set trees. Unluckily, the woods didn't extend all the way back home...

My torch! I flicked it on and tossed it to my right, halting behind a tree so the monster couldn't hunt me by sound. I covered my mouth with my arm to muffle my heavy breathing.

The monster veered off toward the fallen torch.

I knew I couldn't kill the beast with a stone, but perhaps I could convince it to return to a waiting meal instead of chasing me further. I squatted to gather a handful of rocks. Silently mouthing a prayer, I hurled a stone at the beast's eyes. My throw missed high and to the right.

The Lyon snarled.

I threw again with all my adrenaline-powered strength, but trembling spoiled my aim.

Roaring, the Lyon loped toward me, its claws tearing out chunks of sod.

My heart thundered in my chest. I had time only for one final attempt.

I threw. *Clang!*

The stone struck the metal box attached to the monster's

head. Two small pieces tumbled from the box to the ground.

The Lyon stopped and blinked, shaking its head from side to side. It nodded toward me before retreating.

Was that a nod of thanks? I wondered. After taking a moment to get my shaking under control, I searched the ground for the loose pieces. Eventually, my hand brushed a sharp-edged rectangle. I grabbed it and sprinted home.

As predicted, my parents were not pleased with me being in the Common alone after dark. After accepting my penalty without argument, I was ordered to my room.

Holding it under my desk lamp, I studied the shiny metal rectangle. It had a delicate hinge on one edge. *Is this a battery cover?* I asked myself. *Did I knock loose a battery?*

Imprinted on the reverse side was "Dstl." A Web search turned up, "The Defence Science and Technology Laboratory (Dstl) is the science inside UK defence and security." *How odd,* I thought, but at that point, exhaustion overtook my curiosity.

꧁ ꧂ ꧁

At breakfast, a newspaper headline caught my eye, "More Sightings of Odd Animal." In the article, the London Zoo confirmed all their animals were accounted for. And a

Dstl spokesman denied the MOD was conducting genetic experiments on animals.

I smirked. Technically, it wouldn't be genetic experimentation if the Defence Ministry had captured the Stratford Lyon and attached a mind-control device.

※ ※ ※

Once I was no longer grounded, I resumed hiking on the Common. To my great relief, I no longer discovered beheaded animals. Had the Lyon returned to its legendary home in Hampshire's New Forest?

Regardless, I felt joy at having protected the animals of Wimbledon Common. I never again visited after dark—better safe than sorry. And I vowed to stay well away from New Forest. One encounter with the Stratford Lyon was quite enough for a lifetime.

Henry Herz's speculative fiction short stories include "Out, Damned Virus" (*Daily Science Fiction*), "Bar Mitzvah on Planet Latke" (*Coming of Age*, Albert Whitman & Co.), "The Magic Backpack" (Metastellar), "Unbreakable" (*Musing of the Muses*, Brigid's Gate Press), "The Case of the Murderous Alien" (*Spirit Machine*, Air and Nothingness Press), "The Ghosts of Enerhodar" (*Literally Dead*, Alienhead Press), "Maria & Maslow" (*Highlights for Children*), and "A Proper Party" (*Ladybug Magazine*). He's edited five anthologies and written twelve picture books, including the critically acclaimed *I Am Smoke*. www.henryherz.com.

Trigger Tree
by Carl Papa Palmer

een must be quiet, so quiet,

listen, stay very still, listen

not attract attention,

their attention

ween must remain very quiet

beginning, beginning to happen, happen again, happening
again, arising, me, the ween,
ween is again rising, rising from the depths, quietness of the
deep, my home,

this ween, this, this thing, me, what can I be? what? this, this ween, me, the ween, alive,

not life people know, ween, once, long past, there were

many, many weens, happy weens,

people, people came, invaded with houses, and weens died,

no reason, just died, only one,

me, the ween, blessed, cursed, hallowed

I arise, muttering, remembering, repeating, that noise of

people, their noise, this noise,

Trigger Tree, words I remember, their words, why? why

ween has to go, must go, leave

my home, to where I must go, *Trigger Tree, Trigger Tree*

close, not far, near where I am now, right over there, a

house, houses, houses with people,

many people, people, cause of death, death to weens,

enemy, people, but people hold the

cure, cure for death, death to weens, I fear, fear is present,

ween knows, the hallowed ween

knows, ween must approach, *Trigger Tree*, to receive the

cure, the sweetness of life, cure,

enough cure to last, to last another year, the cure. *Trigger*

Tree, Trigger Tree ween repeats,

repeats faster, faster, ween remembers, ween regrets, if only

ween knew before, before all

the weens, peaceful weens, quiet weens, all weens, died but

me, died, leaving me alone, so

all alone, to, to what? and why? why must people, *Trigger*

Tree, Trigger Tree, Trigger Tree,

now again, again the hallowed ween make the journey, to

the house, to the houses, the many

houses, house after house, as last year, year before, previous

year, the year before that, the

ween, the ween approaches, carefully approaches that first

house, *Trigger Tree*, ween hears,

house is surrounded by running, running, loudness, noises,

Trigger Tree, Trigger Tree, people,

large, small, all yelling *Trigger Tree, Trigger Tree*, dressed

as ghosts, goblins, ghouls, monsters,

vampires, *Trigger Tree*, some ween sized, some appearing

to be a ween, not unlike a ween,

noises, loudness, *Trigger Tree*, screamed in many voices,

ween hears again, *Trigger Tree*,

Trigger Tree, loud, afraid. determined, he, he must, must go

to the house, but, but the first house

is always worst, ween moves, he mutters, *Trigger Tree*,

people, loud, running, ween says louder,

Trigger Tree Ween moves among, amidst, amongst, with

the people, closer, moving closer, closer

to the house, noises, loudness, afraid, the house opens,

louder, so loud, the voices, in unison they

scream, ween screams, together, together they all scream,

Trigger Tree, *Trigger Tree*, *Trigger Tree*,

The Cure! The cure is issued, the cure for death, the

sweetness of life, mine, ween is saved, in my

grasp, the cure, ween has the cure, I am now the Happy

Hallowed Ween, *Trigger Tree*.

Carl "Papa" Palmer of Old Mill Road in Ridgeway, Virginia, lives in University Place, Washington. He is retired from the military and Federal Aviation Administration (FAA), enjoying life as "Papa" to his grand descendants and being a Franciscan Hospice volunteer.
PAPA's MOTTO: Long Weekends Forever!

The Puppet Men
by Steven Lord

If you go down to the Common,

To splash around in the rain,

You'd better watch out for the puppet men,

Or you'll never be seen again.

They'll tie you up, they'll cut you up,

And they'll eat up all... your... BRAINS!

"Mum! MUM! Freddie's being horrible again!"

Tabitha could feel the tears prickling at the sides of her eyes as her brother sang his nasty little song, but she blinked them away before they could escape into the sunlight. She knew that crying would just encourage him to keep going.

Her mum looked down at them for a moment. "Leave your sister alone, Freddie," she muttered before turning her attention back to her mobile phone. She spent so much time looking at that little screen that Tabitha sometimes wondered how she didn't walk into things. Tabitha missed the way mum used to be. She missed the mum that had spent whole mornings with her, the one who had read her lovely stories and sat down to tea parties with her and her dolls. Those had been happy days.

Even Freddie had been nicer back then, teaching her how to ride her bike and playing games. Hide and seek had always been her favourite; she remembered the excitement of running away into the corridors, trying to find a hiding spot while Freddie shouted out the numbers. There were loads of great sneaky places in their old house—antique beds with tall metal frames to crawl under, huge wooden wardrobes that reached up to the high ceilings, even toy chests big enough for her to fit into.

That all changed when Dad went away. They had to move from that big old house in the countryside to their new flat in London. Mum didn't play with them anymore—in fact, she barely even spoke to them. And Freddie had turned into the nastiest big brother there ever was, all pinches and elbows. His favourite trick was telling scary stories. Deep down, Tabitha knew they weren't real, but they still frightened her, especially late at night when the lights went out and she was left all alone in the dark. Even now, in the grey light of the rainy autumn day, she was a little bit nervous.

The three of them were walking through a narrow path in the woods. A chilly breeze was blowing through the air, rustling the treetops and making the branches on either side of the path bend to and fro. The movement kept catching her eye as shadows flitted across her face like tiger stripes. Was that just the leaves moving in the wind? Or was someone there, following them?

"The puppet men are real, you know." Freddie was looking at her with serious eyes, but she could see a little twist in his lips, like he was trying to hold back a smirk. "They told us about them in school. They live here in Wimbledon Common, and they snatch naughty little children."

"Well, you'd better watch out then," Tabitha said, a

frown wrinkling her forehead. "You're mean, and I bet they try to get you first."

"No, they prefer little girls. They're tastier."

Tabitha looked up at her mum, fear and dismay in her eyes. But her mum hadn't noticed. She wouldn't care anyway; she was too busy on her phone. That was all she seemed to care about these days.

All of a sudden, they turned a bend in the path and the foliage around them opened up into a round clearing, with a single old oak tree sat in the middle of the circle. Squirrels scampered in the grass and ran up and down the side of the tree like crazy yo-yos. Tabitha could feel a smile creeping onto her face for the first time in ages.

"Great, we're here," her mum said. "I'll get the picnic ready. You two go off and play while I'm setting up." And with that, she headed off to the oak tree to set down her rucksack.

Freddie didn't look happy with the thought of having to play with his little sister. Then, as Tabitha watched, his scowl turned into a grin. "I know," he said. "Let's play hide and seek."

"Yes," Tabitha cried, almost jumping up and down in

excitement.

"I'll count to one hundred. You hide," he said, then before she could answer, he closed his eyes and started counting loudly. "One. Two. Three."

Tabitha looked around, her eyes dashing from one direction to the other. There was nowhere obvious to hide in the clearing—the only object in sight was the big oak tree, and it was too big for her to climb. Then she noticed a little path off to her left, cutting through some brambles. It was just high enough for her to squeeze down, but Freddie would never manage it. It was perfect.

She scampered across to the entrance of the little trail. Thorny brambles arched tightly across the top of the path at her head height, making it look more like a tunnel than a natural break in the foliage. As she looked down the trail, the grass, so lush and green in the clearing, turned brown and dingy before it faded away into hard soil so dark it was almost red. Tabitha started to have second thoughts about her hiding place.

Then she heard Freddie's call from across the green. "Eighty-one. Eighty-two." She didn't have long left—it was now or never. She took a deep breath, ducked her head, and headed down the strange little path.

After a few minutes, she noticed how quiet everything had become. Wimbledon Common looked like the countryside, but it wasn't really. You could always hear the sound of cars driving along the busy London roads, and airplanes flying overhead on their way to Heathrow Airport just a few miles to the north. But now, all that background noise had vanished. She had got used to the constant roar of the city over the last few months, even though she preferred the peace and quiet of the countryside. Now the noise had gone, she kind of missed it—the deathly silence was a bit scary.

She took a deep breath and continued down the dark path, keen to get away from the clearing. By now, Freddie would be searching for her. Jagged branches seemed to reach out to her from left and right, long, wicked thorns catching on her jacket and trousers, slowing her down. She pressed on for another few minutes as the path got narrower and narrower until she could go no further. Ahead was nothing but dense bramble. With difficulty, she managed to turn around, but when she tried to head back up the path, the prickly branches held her tight. She was stuck.

She could feel her heart race, quick, short breaths whipping in and out of her mouth like a panting dog. Her thoughts became foggy as panic flooded her mind. What would she do? What if Freddie couldn't find her? What if he wasn't even looking for her? He might have been joking about hide and seek—it was exactly the kind of nasty thing he would do. She might be stuck here forever.

Then a memory flashed into her head. She had a vision of her old teacher, Mrs Gallagher, sitting down with her just before she left the countryside and moved to London. In sympathetic tones, she had explained how difficult the next few months would be.

"Now Tabitha," she'd said. "There are going to be lots of changes coming up, some of them good and some of them bad. London can be a scary place. It's alright to be scared, but the problem is that when you're scared, you can't really think properly. So, if you do find yourself in a scary situation, I want you to do this for me. Close your eyes and take a deep breath. Hold it for a second. Then let it out and say 'I can do this'. You'll feel much better."

Just thinking of the old lady, familiar and comforting like apple pie on a Sunday, made Tabitha feel a little better. She decided to give it a go. This was definitely a scary situation, after all. She squeezed her eyes shut, took a big breath through her mouth, and then let it go. "I can do this," she said into the darkness.

It worked. Her mind started to clear, her thoughts whirring instead of being stuck in a muddy puddle of fear. She wasn't stuck—her jacket was! She wriggled, bending her arms backwards so they would slide through the sleeves. They were half out when a flash of movement off to the right caught her eye.

She turned her head to see a sight out of her worst nightmares. A tiny skeleton, no more than four feet tall, was jerking towards her out of the brambles. The bones were grey as stone, but some yellow and red rags still fluttered from the shoulders and hips. Worst of all was how it moved. The legs and arms were jerking up and down like the puppets in a Punch and Judy show. "The puppet man," Tabitha whispered, dread in her voice.

The little skeleton danced its way closer. To her surprise, it collapsed into a pile of bones a couple of feet in front of her; the skull sitting neatly upright on top. She noticed for the first time that the top of the skull had been sliced off.

Things got worse.

From the open top of the skull, a finger appeared. Then another, and another, followed by a hand, then an arm. It made no sense—the skull was only three or four inches across at most, yet somehow a full-sized man was emerging from within. In a few seconds, the man was out, standing in front of Tabitha with a horrible grin on his face. His whole body was bright red and his eyes gleamed with yellow fire. In his right hand he gripped a wicked knife, the sharp steel edge catching what little light remained in the dark path.

Tabitha closed her eyes. "I can do this."

She could hear the man advancing towards her. He spoke, his voice scratchy and dusty, like old gravestones. "How nice to see you," he croaked. "I need a new body. My old one was falling apart. And yours looks perfect."

"I can do this!"

She could feel the warm, foetid breath of the man on her face now. He whispered straight into Tabitha's ear. "My friends and I have been waiting for so long for new puppets."

"I CAN DO THIS!" she screamed, yanking her arms out of the sleeves. She barrelled forward, taking the man by surprise. He toppled backwards as she shot past, her legs pumping like they had never before. She ran and ran, ignoring the fire in her lungs, until after what felt like an eternity, she finally popped out into the clearing. She looked around frantically until she spotted her mum, still pottering by the tree, Freddie by her side. A picnic blanket lay spread out by her feet, some plates and cups dotted on top.

"Mum!" she cried.

"What's wrong, my love?" her mother asked, concern in her voice. "Come here, everything's alright now."

"No, no. You don't understand, we have to go. Now!"

Her mother looked at her strangely. Then she smiled. "Of course, darling. If that's what you want, that's what we'll do."

Freddie beamed at her. "Yes, let's go."

Tabitha almost fainted with happiness. She set off, not wanting to be in that cursed wood for one second longer than she needed to be. After a minute, she glanced back to make sure they were following her.

They were right behind her. As they walked, their arms and legs jerked up and down.

Like puppets.

Steven Lord is a fantasy and sci-fi author from the UK. After leaving university, he spent 16 years travelling the world, meeting interesting people. He has seen the sun setting in the Himalayas, dust storms rolling through the deserts of Afghanistan, hurricanes tearing through the Caribbean and icebergs drifting in the South Atlantic. Since 2019, he has settled down a bit, taking advantage of the change of pace to follow a long-held ambition to write fiction. His influences include Neal Stephenson, Stephen King and Iain M Banks. Steven currently lives in London with his wife, dog and two cats and is resigned to his place at the bottom of the pecking order in the house...
Find Steven on Facebook at @StevenLordAuthor.

Mischievous Deeds
by Maggie D. Brace

Stag beetles scamper upon the heath
where highway men once trod.
Now lazy picnickers lie beneath
asleep upon the sod.

An otherworld lies near the bog,
unbeknownst to men,
who heedlessly walk their dog
and tumble into the fen.

Lurking amidst the pen ponds,

wee fairy folk lie in wait,

they slip from their fae bonds

to gather at garden gate.

Planning their mischievous deeds,

they gambol and caper away.

Hiding betwixt the sedge and reeds,

they giggle away the day.

All escapades and pulling pranks

they wile away the hours,

pushing tourists down grassy banks

and pulling the heads off flowers.

Hiding stinkweed in the heath

and tripping up the runners,

sprinkling itch powder beneath

and butter atop the sunners.

Their naughty day is over too soon.

The faeries fly home for bed.

Lying below the crescent moon,

plotting their next day of dread.

Maggie D. Brace, a life-long denizen of Maryland, teacher, gardener, basketball player and author attended St. Mary's College, where she met her soulmate, and Loyola University, Maryland. She has written *'Tis Himself: The Tale of Finn MacCool* and *Grammy's Glasses*, and has multiple short works and poems in various anthologies. She remains a humble scrivener and avid reader. @MaggieDBrace

Benefit of the Doubt
by Kevin Hopson

"You can't go," Millie pleaded.

Caitlin sat along the edge of the bed, gawking at her younger sister from across the room.

"Why not?" Caitlin said.

Millie approached. "You know why. The dragon lives there."

"Exactly."

"What does that mean?"

"It means I want to find it," Caitlin clarified.

Millie huffed. "Why would you want to do that? You know the townspeople are angry over their gardens. They're going to hunt the dragon for all the damage it's done."

"Which is why I'm going," Caitlin said. "I'm going to prove that the dragon has had nothing to do with it."

"And what if I tell Mum?" Millie threatened.

"Then I'll tell her about your little accident last week. The broken vase you blamed on Snickers instead."

Snickers was their cat, and the young feline often got into trouble, so the lie had been a believable one.

Millie's brows furrowed and she let out a grunt. "Fine. Go. But don't say I didn't warn you."

🦋 🦋 🦋

Caitlin hopped on her bike and made haste for Queensmere park. It's where the dragon was often spotted. Sometimes drinking from the local pond. Other times venturing through the woodlands that surrounded it.

It was an overcast autumn morning, and Caitlin shivered as the wind at her face gradually turned cooler. The temperatures often dropped when she neared the nature preserve. When she arrived, fog clung to the ground, concealing much of the pond and the woodlands beyond.

Caitlin parked her bike on a dirt trail and walked along

the bank. She inspected the water the best she could, but the fog made seeing difficult. Every now and then, Caitlin would hear a plop in the water. She would immediately come to a stop and scan the surface of the pond.

Instinct told her it was only part of the wildlife. Fish were an obvious culprit. Ducks and geese weren't as abundant as they once were, with a dragon on the prowl, but birds were still a common sight when visiting. And turtles popped up on occasion as well.

People described the dragon as being huge. Vicious. Menacing. She didn't put much trust in their words. However, if the accounts were true, the dragon would likely be much louder in its movement.

She grew tired of the water and made her way up the bank, trekking along the edge of the woodlands that encircled the pond.

"D-R-A-G-O-N," she said.

It felt silly, but Caitlin wasn't sure what else to do. She continued the pattern for several minutes, making her way around the pond and calling out for the dragon every so often. The fog was beginning to burn off, and she spotted her bike ahead.

Caitlin's shoulders slumped in disappointment. She was about to hook a leg over the bike seat when another noise caught her attention. A breaking of twigs. A rustling of leaves. Then a snort came. Something emerged between the trees. A silhouette. One she couldn't quite make out.

When she finally saw it, Caitlin stumbled backwards, landing on her bum. The creature slowly approached, coming to a stop only a couple of metres away. It had four legs and two wings, much like a dragon, but it was covered in brown fur instead of scaly skin. And it was no bigger than a dog. Not the monstrosity many had claimed.

"What do you want?" the dragon snarled.

Caitlin got to her feet and wiped the dirt from her pants. Doubts about coming here crept into her mind.

"I don't care for humans," the dragon said.

Caitlin swallowed. "I'm not afraid of you," she said, with a lack of conviction.

The dragon snickered. "You should be."

Part of her wanted to run, but she couldn't will her feet to move.

"Do you have a name?" she asked, attempting to ease the tension.

He let out a breath, and Caitlin felt the warm air brush her face.

"Jierso," he finally said. "But why do you care?"

Caitlin ignored the question.

"I'm Caitlin," she said, looking him over. "You're not what I expected."

"What does that mean?" he roared.

She flinched, then shook her head. "Nothing. You're just different than what I imagined. It's not a bad thing."

Jierso's mouth parted, revealing several sharp teeth. "Why are you here? I'm hungry and would like to eat."

Caitlin cringed at the thought. Was he planning to eat her? If so, her back was to the water, and she had no place to go.

"I want to help you," she said, hoping to sway the dragon.

"Help?" he said. "Why? And How?"

"The townsfolk are angry over their gardens. Most of them have been destroyed. And they blame you for it. They're going to hunt you down and kill you."

"And why do they think I have anything to do with that?"

"Because they're human. They fear things they don't

understand."

Jierso eventually nodded. "Perhaps I underestimated you. You seem wiser than most."

"Is it true?" Caitlin asked. "That you haven't played a part in any of this?"

When the dragon refused to answer, Caitlin's heart sank. She wanted to believe that Jierso was an innocent victim. Even if he showed aggression towards humans, he had good reason for it.

Jierso took a breath, and his stern expression began to fade. He pondered for a moment. "Have you ever heard of lily beetles?"

Caitlin's eyes narrowed. "I don't think so. Why?"

"They're not native to these parts. They're what you call an invasive species. Lily beetles were brought here many years ago, and they've multiplied in numbers ever since."

"What do they do?" 

"They eat certain flowers, such as lilies. Hence their name. If I had to wager a guess, I'd say they're to blame for all of this."

"But what do lily beetles have to do with you?" Caitlin said.

"They're a source of food for me. It takes hundreds of them to fill my belly, but I eat them whenever I can."

Caitlin took a step forward. "Then you're actually helping the town. You're not doing harm. You're doing good."

"But who's going to believe it?" Jierso said.

"I'll go back and tell everyone," Caitlin replied. "I'll make them see the truth."

"I'm afraid it will take more than your word to convince them."

"Maybe they'll believe me," a voice said.

Caitlin turned to look. A figure appeared. A woman. But not just any woman.

"Mum!" Caitlin said.

Caitlin would give Millie an earful when she got back, but it was a relief to see her mum nonetheless.

"How long have you been standing there?" Caitlin asked.

"Long enough to hear your conversation," she replied. "It took every bit of my willpower not to intervene. You always try to see the good in everything. Much like me. If I'd screamed at you and hauled you away for your actions, I'd only be a hypocrite."

Caitlin appreciated the gesture and kind words. "Do you think it will work? Telling people what Jierso has told us?"

"Sometimes humans don't need a reason to fight," Jierso interrupted. "They'll want to hunt me just for being a dragon."

"Maybe," Caitlin's mum said. "But if we fail to persuade the town, it won't be for a lack of trying." She looked at Caitlin. "Come on. We can put your bike in my car."

Caitlin made her way to her mum's side, glancing back at Jierso.

"If they can't be persuaded to leave me alone," Jierso said, "tell them I'll hunt them down and eat them."

Caitlin's mouth hung agape. "What?"

Much to her surprise, Jierso offered a smile. And not a malevolent smile. A genuine one.

"Sorry," he said. "That was my poor attempt at a joke."

Kevin Hopson has dabbled in many genres over the years, but crime fiction and fantasy are his true loves. His novelette, Pursuing the Dead, was a 2019 Author Shout Reader Ready Awards winner. And if you're a fan of light fantasy, check out The Emperor's Guard series. www.kmhopson.com.

The Plight of the Kerplimes
by Dawn DeGraal

At Wimbledon Common, through my naked eye,

Spotting tall buildings that reach the sky.

Frozen in concrete (they're frozen in time).

Beneath their foundations live the Kerplime.

They live underground, for they can't smell the roses.

They'd drown in the rain from their upside-down noses.

Their small beady eyes are wide in the dark

While they search and they seek the angry land shark.

They hunt down those creatures. They watch, and they wait

Using small Kerplimes they set out as bait.

Only by instinct do they ever feel

The hook and string on a large reel

The bait has been taken, they thrash it about

Turning those land sharks inside to out.

The Kerplime hunter, a lucky fella,

uses the land shark as his umbrella.

Now he sees sunshine and smells the rose.

The umbrella covers his upside-down nose.

But the sharks only last just for a while

And the Kerplimes becomes part of the land shark's smile.

So, on Wimbledon Common you give, and you take

Whatever you have, for goodness' sake.

Don't use a land shark for shelter, you bet.

One minute they're shade, but the next, you'll be wet.

Invited to dinner, they're just the snack.

Beware, oh you Kerplimes, of the land shark's attack

Clueless Kerplimes don't see the big deal

until they've become a land shark's next meal.

Dawn DeBraal lives in rural Wisconsin with her husband Red, two little rescue dogs, and a stray cat. Dawn has published over 300 stories in many online magazines and anthologies, including Palm-sized press, Spillwords, Mercurial Stories, Potato Soup Journal, Edify Fiction, Zimbell House Publishing, Black Hare Press, Clarendon House, Blood Song Books, Fantasia Divinity, Cafelit, Reanimated Writers, The World of Myth, Dastaan World, Vamp Cat, Runcible Spoon, Siren's Call, Setu, Kandisha Press, Terror House Magazine, D & T Publishing, Sammie Sands, Iron Horse Publishing, Impspired Magazine, Black Ink Fiction and was the Falling Star Magazine's 2019 Pushcart nominee. linktr.ee/dawndebraal.

Scientists
by Christy Brown

Dave and Levi ran along the path skirting the Common, dirt kicking up and hitting the backs of their legs as they ran. They dodged walkers on the trail, weaving between them like a game of Mario Kart. Dave's ten-year-old legs had a sizable lead on his brother's six-year-old ones, but Levi was doing his best to keep up.

"Come on, Levi! Freddy is gunna get you if you don't hurry up! He'll eat your toes!"

Levi ran faster and giggled for a moment to show he wasn't afraid, but then snuck a quick look behind him to check for Freddy, the chicken-chomping monster. Dave had told his little brother a story about a green-eyed, drooling monster that haunted the chicken coop at night. In the original story, this monster only ate chickens, but once Dave realised Levi was afraid of Freddy the chicken monster, this drooling beast was suddenly also interested in eating little six-year-old boys.

"I'm coming!" Levi shouted, closing the gap between them.

The boys ran off the main trail, pushing through trees, bushes, and brush to reach the bog. The night before had seen a steady, hard rain, and the boys couldn't hold back the excitement of all the fun creatures they would find today; rain always brought out the good ones. Dave had a glass jar with pre-punched holes all prepared for catching tadpoles. Levi had a plastic tub cleared out for any other grimy little creatures they might find down in the bog. Most days they were just two crazy brothers, but today they were scientists looking for new specimens to study.

Running full speed, Levi reached Dave, passing him as Dave slowed to a light jog. Proud of his advance, Levi turned back to gain his older brother's acknowledgement.

"Look, Dave, I'm so fast! I beat you to the—" But Levi's announcement was cut off, as his foot caught an especially wet patch of mud and slid out from underneath him. Before Dave could move to catch him, Levi was on the ground, covered in mud from head to toe, and the plastic tub he was holding sailed through the air into a patch of overgrown bushes. Dave hesitated a moment, not quite knowing how to react, then doubled over with laughter, almost dropping his tadpole jar.

"Hey! Don't laugh at me!" Levi scolded, as he picked himself up off the ground without making a single effort to brush off the mud. He immediately scanned the brush for his plastic container, beginning to grow worried he'd have nothing to hold his creatures, and therefore not be a real scientist. He pushed aside branches, stuck his head into the brush, and even tried to climb in to get a better look: no luck.

Finding nothing, he hung his head and turned back to his brother.

"Dave! I can't find my bucket!"

Dave rolled his eyes, turned his back on his brother, and headed in the direction of the bog.

"Not my problem, little booger," he said. Then began his tadpole hunt.

Levi's shoulders slumped forward, his head bowed, and

he followed his older brother down to the bog—bucketless. He stood on the edge of the water, watching as Dave trudged into the muck up to his knees and thrust his arm down into the water, scooping up a large group of tadpoles. Dave was a scientist on a very important mission, and Levi envied his older brother.

Turning back to Levi, Dave held out the glass jar at eye level. "And the young David arrives at the scene to collect his specimens, which he will soon take back to the lab, cut them open, and create a cure for all the sicknesses of the world!" Dave shouted, raising the jar into the air and following up with a menacing, evil laugh. "Muahahaha!"

"But what about me, Dave? What will I be?" Levi asked.

Dave hesitated, then turned to his little brother, scrunching his face up into a large, grinch-like smile. "You're just the scientist's annoying little brother that lost the specimen bucket."

Levi's lower lip curled outward as his eyes began to water. Then he rubbed his face with his dirty little hands, pulled his lips in tightly, and shouted back at his brother, "Fine! I don't want to be a scientist with you, anyway!"

Turning his back on the mean scientist, Levi began to

walk back up to the trail.

"Whatever, you'll just have to look out for Freddy all by yourself," Dave yelled.

For a moment, Levi hesitated, but only for a moment. Then, he folded his arms across his chest and stomped back up toward the trail, away from the bog, and out of sight.

Dave was far too caught up in his scientific work to care that Levi had left him there alone—he'd make it home eventually. Besides, Levi really had been a little brat. He'd lost the darn specimen bucket!

Holding his glass jar up to the sunlight, Dave tried to count his tadpoles, but was startled by a grumble from the bush behind him. Dave's heart began to thump in his chest, and he was suddenly sorry he had allowed his brother to leave him alone. He shifted his gaze back toward the shrubs, eyes wide.

"Who…who's there?" Dave asked.

There was no answer, but he caught the movement of leaves within the bushes and knew he wasn't alone. He quickly screwed the lid onto his glass jar—he couldn't allow his tadpoles to escape—and attempted to run back up towards the path. He had a moment of alarm as his foot caught in the same wet patch of mud Levi had slid in, and down he went. Lying on his back, covered in wet slop, he heard the noise once again, and, once again, he turned to look at the shrubs, head nestled in a wet clod of dirt.

This time, a small man stepped out from the covering.

Still lying in the mud, Dave's mouth dropped open as he studied this strange creature. It had a long, white beard, a tall pointy hat, and small pointy shoes. Dave thought it must be an elf, or maybe a gnome. The strangest thing about the small man was, of course, his size. The tiny fella stood only about as tall as a chicken. Dave had never seen such a creature. Not in real life, anyway.

"Get outta here!" shouted the little man, eyebrows narrowing tightly into a scowl.

Dave started as he heard these sharp words come from this little man, and all of a sudden, he wished he had not been so mean to his little brother. Dave moved his hands at the speed of a snail, trying not to startle the small man, and pushed them into the mud as he lifted himself into a sitting position.

"Ya can't hear, boy?" The small man with the stiff face shouted, "I told ya ta git!"

Dave shuddered and tried to answer, "I…I…um."

"Ah! Ya dumb as a rock ya are." The man's eyebrows softened, his face began to relax, and a small smile grew where the scowl had been.

Dave noted the small man's change in tone, and his fear began to ease. "I'm David. I…I just came to play in the water and—"

"And to find ya some tadpoles, uh?" The small man's face crumpled into a sneer as he said this, and his words caused Dave to shrink back again in fear.

"Yes…sir? I was just playing a game with my brother. We—"

"Let me just tell ya, my lad, that stealin' and harmin' the life in this bog will set down a curse upon ya." With this, the small man tilted his chin downward and raised his eyebrows at Dave. Dave didn't know a lot about curses, but he knew it was some sort of dark spell that makes bad things happen, and he certainly didn't want that.

"I-I don't want a curse," said Dave, lowering his eyes to his tadpole collection, "but I got these…and they're mine. I can't just let them go. I'm a scientist!"

The small man dropped one eyebrow, raised his hand to

his beard, and thought for a moment. Then, a slight smile grew on his face, and he said, "I'll make ya an offer. I'll leave ya ta play yer game, and all ya have to do is let me play too!" The small man's lips curled up into a sharp grin, and one eyebrow raised in a question.

Dave thought for a moment and considered the little man's offer. The creature didn't appear to be angry, and Levi had left Dave to play here all on his own. Dave felt he certainly deserved a friend to play with. Levi was supposed to have been a scientist also, but he ran off like a little baby when he lost his bucket.

"How can you be a scientist without a bucket for your specimens?" Dave said, raising an eyebrow at the little man.

The little man held up a finger, then turned and disappeared back into the bush. A second later, he returned, holding Levi's lost bucket. Dave's face lit up in a smile, and he accepted the little man's terms.

Letting out a wicked giggle, the man waved his hand in a circular motion, and Dave began to feel dizzy.

The smile on the small man's face began to grow and grow until Dave felt the smile had outgrown the man's face. Then, it seemed as if the man's face was growing to catch up with the enormous smile, and before Dave knew what was happening, the small man wasn't so small anymore.

The world had grown, and Dave's stomach felt weak; his head was a dizzy blur, and his insides would soon be on the outside if the spinning didn't stop. David closed his eyes and took in slow, deep breaths. Once his stomach relaxed and the world stopped spinning, Dave opened his eyes to a very different world.

He still lay on the ground, much like before, only now he lay wriggling in the wet mud with no arms and no legs. The world stood towering over him, and everything was huge! The small man, who was now a giant man, walked towards him, laughing that menacing laugh.

"Now I'm the scientist and you're the tadpole! Isn't this a fun game?" he said.

Levi sat on a bench, legs curled up into his chest, tears dried against his warm cheeks. He was trying to remember why he had got mad, why he had left Dave alone, and couldn't.

He was bored.

He hopped off the bench and made his way back down to the bog. When he got there, he was saddened to find Dave was not there. Noticing the glass jar sitting in the mud, he walked over to the water.

Dave wouldn't leave his specimen jar here, thought Levi as he reached the bog.

Levi's face shrivelled up into a frown as he realised what was in the jar. There was a tadpole—just one.

Why would Dave capture just one tadpole, then leave it here to die in the sun?

Levi shrugged his shoulders, then noticed his small plastic bucket lying near the shrubs.

"Yes!" he shouted. "Now I can be a scientist!"

Levi scooped up his bucket, then skipped off in search of more critters.

Leaving the tadpole in the jar.

To die in the sun.

Christy Brown lives in the United States; she is from California, and currently lives in Virginia with her husband and 8 children. She is a high school English teacher and navy veteran. She enjoys writing stories inspired by her children and her surroundings.

Night on the Common
by D.J. Tyrer

Child wanders out one evening

    (Unnoticed by parents or passersby)

    Onto Wimbledon Common

In search of furry recyclers

But, instead of fiction, finds fact

What really lurks on the Common

In the deep shadows of the night

Long-limbed and loping

Humanoid, but not human

Remnant of an elder world

Old when England was young

And hungry—so hungry

Reaches out for the child

Wriggling fingers snatching at hair

Tugging tufts from scalp, painful

Terrifying, horrid troll-thing

With the appetite of ages

Desires to devour, munch, eat

Child runs, shrieking, screaming

Runs home to bed

Hides under covers, cowers

Hoping, just hoping

The troll-thing cannot leave the Common

Cannot follow her home

Below, she hears the back door open

Child holds her breath

Waits…

D.J. Tyrer is the person behind Atlantean Publishing, and has been published in The Rhysling Anthology 2016, and issues of Cyaegha, Enchanted Conversation, The Horrorzine, Illumen, Scifaikuest, Sirens Call, Spectral Realms, and Star*Line. SuperTrump and A Wuhan Whodunnit are available to download from the Atlantean Publishing website.

Merlin, Me, and the Shiny Noollab
by A.H. Syme

I woke up to Merlin meowing and nudging my head.

"What?" I mumbled sleepily and turned on my side.

"Meow," Merlin said, and this time it was loud.

"Cut it out, Merlin. You will wake everyone up," I said crossly, sitting up in my bed.

Merlin jumped down and ran to the door and then back.

I could see the door was ajar, so why didn't Merlin go out? I scratched my head and then my chin. Yawned a big yawn and swung my feet to the floor.

Merlin rushed to the door and back again.

"I get it, Merlin," I whispered, putting on my slippers. "You want me to follow."

Merlin meowed again, and I followed the big, fluffy, orange cat out into the hallway. The wooden floorboards creaked as I stepped on them, so I tiptoed as best as I could after my cat.

Merlin had shown up at our house one day and had stayed. I begged and pleaded with Mum and Dad to keep him. Dad wasn't keen. I could tell he was getting fed up with me begging when he called me Thomasina. Yuck 'n' double yuck, I don't like my name. That is why I make everyone call me Tom. Mum and Dad only use Thomasina when I'm in trouble or being annoying.

Occasionally, I do have lapses and get what I call Ben-yike-tis! Like appendicitis, only worse, and I act silly like my pesky 6-year-old brother, Ben. Sometimes I think he is contagious, like the flu or a bothersome itch.

The good news was Mum said we could keep Merlin if nobody came to claim him. Luckily, no one did. So Merlin settled in, and now the cat with the big 'M' on his forehead rules the household. Well, I mean me. He seems to enjoy bossing ten-year-old girls like me around. While he always keeps a close watch with his strange eyes on Ben.

Merlin has odd eyes. One eye is a golden colour, and the other is a blue colour. I thought he looked magical, like a wizard, and picked Merlin for his name. It goes with his big ginger 'M' mark. Ben wanted to call him Super Ninja Tiger Warrior or Killer Cat because he should be a superhero's cat. Mum liked the name Butterbean. She seems to have a peculiar interest in butter beans because she keeps serving them up and trying to get them in our mouths. Dad said we should call him King Pin because he acts like royalty.

Happily, I won all the rock-paper-scissors games, and Merlin became Merlin. Mum and Dad said "Well done", but Ben blew a raspberry, making a big farty noise. I didn't care. I was just glad that Merlin could stay.

Now, I followed Merlin, tiptoeing quietly across the rug in our hall. I did not want to wake up Mum, but I didn't have to worry about Dad because he was away on a work trip again. Dad is a space scientist and works in space technology. He can read all the signals we send and receive from Earth's space probes around Saturn, Jupiter, Mars, and other faraway planets. Dad is good at his job and sometimes has to go to America to help with their space projects.

Merlin stopped at Ben's door. I sneaked up beside him and pushed the door open. The first thing I saw was an empty bed. The window was open, and the moonlight shone through onto Ben's pillow. It was bright enough for me to see the red rockets and white stars on Ben's duvet; it lay in a lump at the bottom of the bed.

The duvet looked strange. Like the twisted body of a beast was lying underneath, waiting for someone to pull back the cover so it could attack. A dark shadow moved across the bed. I jumped, and my heart thumped quickly, pounding up and down like a toad trying to win a race. Something was under that duvet, and it wasn't Ben. I backed away slowly; my mouth was dry, but my hands were sweaty. My stomach was so tense it felt like a thousand rubber bands were being pulled tightly inside it.

I was about to turn and run when Merlin rushed in and jumped on the duvet. Nothing. The duvet collapsed down, and another shadow slipped across the floor. Crikey Dickey. What a gooseneck I am. It was clouds moving across the moon's face and partly blocking its light that made the shadows. My heart slowed down to its usual beat, and my tummy wasn't tight anymore.

"Thanks, Merlin," I whispered.

I shouldn't let my imagination get the better of me. Mum said I let it run wild, but I don't think Mum knows what my mind is like because I don't even keep it on a lead. I told myself to calm down. Ben was probably up to one of his dumb tricks.

I checked under the bed. Sometimes Ben did silly things like that, hiding under beds and in wardrobes. Once, he hid in an old sack down in the basement. Unfortunately, the sack was hessian, a rough, bristly fabric that made Ben itch, scratch, and wiggle about inside the sack.

Dad had come into the basement, and seeing something moving about in the sack, he thought it might be rats. So, he picked up his shovel and was about to swing it hard at the bag when suddenly Ben's head popped out.

Dad got such a shock his face turned white, and his mouth hung open. He looked like a zombie who had just found out it's a zombie. Dad dropped the shovel and grabbed Ben up and hugged him hard, then told him off for being in the basement. I got told off and sent to my room for letting Ben be in the basement.

Now that is so unfair! I mean, no one looks where someone is going when playing hide-and-seek unless the person is a cheat. I am not a cheat, but after that, I sometimes peek to see which way Ben is going. It helps me find Ben quicker, but I do it just to be sure he is safe. Really, truly.

I opened his wardrobe—no Ben. I checked everywhere—no Ben. Merlin left the bed, leapt up onto the windowsill, and looked out the window. I hurried over, and my heart nearly stopped. This time it felt like my heart had turned to stone, like a huge lump of rock that sat hard and solid in my chest. Breathe, I told myself, but I could hardly take in any air. Below me, walking out of our backyard and into Wimbledon Common, was Ben.

I could see he was following something that looked like a balloon that floated in the air in front of him. It was silver and sparkled in the moonlight like a thousand stars were trapped inside it. I have never seen anything like it before. A golden thread hung down from it, and it swung gently back and forth in front of Ben's face.

Then I noticed Ben seemed to walk weirdly. I mean, my

brother is weird, but not that weird. His body was stiff, and his arms were straight down by his side. He walked as if he was under a spell or like he was hypnotised.

Ben walked like a robot. A robot wearing blue pyjamas with little green monkeys and purple dinosaurs all over them. He wore his yellow slippers on his feet.

Crikey Dickey. It was all revolting. I was thinking how disgusting Ben's fashion choices were when Merlin hissed at me, snapping me out of my brain freeze or my pyjama fright. I wasn't sure which one it was, but the good news was my heart felt like it was beating again. Thank goodness.

I hurried to my bedroom and grabbed my robe. I was going to get Mum, but Merlin meowed at my feet and then darted down the stairs. I followed as quickly and as quietly as I could. There was no time to leave Mum a note because I could see the cat flap swinging. I knew Merlin was following Ben, and I had to keep up.

We are lucky because Wimbledon Common is our second backyard, and Ben was walking into it. It is a massive area of 1,100 acres. I mean, that's like a hundred thousand McDonald's stores all in the one place, and millions and millions of hamburgers, and that's not counting the pickles.

It would be easy to get lost—or get a stomachache.

There is woodland, ponds, open land, many trails, and grass areas where teams play sports in this vast natural conservation area. There is also a bog. I shivered. I didn't want Ben going anywhere near the bog or the ponds. He was no good in water and couldn't swim yet. I thought he was unwilling to learn because he connected water with soap. Mum said that was nonsense, but I don't think so. I've seen his knees and elbows, and once, yuck, his butt. It all looked like it needed a good scrub to me.

Wimbledon Common is a great place to explore, play, exercise in and do cartwheels. Many birds, plants and animals live there, but it is not a good place for children to wander around at night.

Rosen Winterbottom, sometimes called Frozen Butt by some nasty boys, reckons strange creatures live in the Commons. He said he had seen a black, hairy thing as big as a man. I thought he was crazy, but as I followed Merlin onto the Commons, I wondered if Frozen Butt—I mean Rosen— might be right.

Dark shadows seemed to move between the trees. I thought I saw something with long arms reaching out towards me, wanting to hold and squeeze me tight. So tight that it would make my skin burst, my eyeballs pop and my bones break one by one. Snap, snap, snap, like dry twigs. Suddenly there was a loud snap behind me, and I ran as fast as I could and hid behind a tree.

My heart was beating so fast it seemed to boom in my ears, and my throat and lungs felt like they were on fire. Worse, a sharp stabbing pain made my face twist in agony. Something touched my legs. I tried to scream but couldn't; I had no breath left. My lungs were burning, and my side felt like it was getting stabbed with a sharp knife. I looked down and…

"Meow," Merlin said.

"Oh, Merlin," I whispered.

Merlin rubbed himself across my shins, and amazingly, I calmed down. I realised it was because I was running so fast and taking great gulps of air that my throat and lungs felt like they were on fire. The stabbing pain was a stitch in my side. It was my wild imagination again, going berserk and thinking about monsters. Talk about scaring myself to death.

Merlin stopped rubbing my legs, lowered his head, and trotted further into the woods. Ahead, I could see Ben standing still in front of the strange floating object. As I got closer, I noticed it was like a balloon but with a shiny, reflective, glass-like surface.

I rushed up to Ben and grabbed his arm.

"Come on," I said.

He didn't move. He was stuck to the spot. A robot that had stopped.

"Don't touch him," a deep voice said.

I jumped and looked around, but nobody was there, only shadows and trees. My hand reached for Ben again.

"Stop," said the voice. A voice that sounded like a woman's voice but deep. "You will hurt him. I will get him out. It just takes a little time."

"Wh-wh-who are you?" I asked, my voice shaky.

"She sounds like an owl," a squeaky voice said.

I was sure I heard a giggle.

"Quiet, Zek," Deep-voice said.

My heart started to flutter as quick as a tongue over ice cream.

"We are visitors from outer space, and we…er…yadiloh here," Deep-voice said.

"Yadiloh?" I repeated, puzzled.

"Yes. You know, when everyone has an easy, relaxing time away from home," Deep- voice said.

"Oh, holidays," I said.

Aha! Yadiloh was "holiday" backwards. I felt a little braver.

"Yes, syadiloh. We come from a moon behind one of Saturn's moons. We are Lunasplotch. And I'm sorry to say my nerdlihc let their noollab go.

Wow, I had a bit to work out with two backward words. So, I scratched my head and then my chin.

"Nerdlihc, ch- children?" I said.

"Yes," said Deep-voice.

"Noollab, Balloon," I said, feeling proud but still a little scared.

"No. Not balloon. A Noollab is a Noollab," Zek said.

Oh. Of course it is. I nodded and glanced at my brother. He was coming out of the spell, or whatever it was he was in.

"We know all about you and your family," Deep-voice said.

"Your father mucks up our vision once every eight months with his signals," said Zek.

"Vision? Like television?" I asked.

"Kind of, yes. So, our mother and father always bring us gnipmac here," Zek said.

"Camping, here," I said, amazed.

This was incredible. I apologised for my dad spoiling their vision viewing.

Deep-voice explained that a Noollab filmed everything in the environment like our CCTV. It then sent the live images back to the children while identifying and explaining what it was. It was a kid's toy. Deep-voice also said the Noollab had an inbuilt safety piece. Unfortunately, it was damaged when her child had fallen and pulled it to the ground. The broken part had the job of finding, rounding up, and bringing home missing Lunasplotch children. Unluckily, the broken Noollab had mistaken Ben for a Lunasplotch.

"But Ben isn't an al…." I was going to say alien, but I thought it might sound rude.

"Isn't a Lunasplotch," I said quickly.

"Well, no. But here, take a look," Deep-voice said.

The air shimmered around me.

"Crikey Dickey!" I said, stunned.

In front of me stood three Lunasplotches. They looked

sort of like humans. Two were about my height, four-and-one-half feet tall, or 138 centimetres, and the other was taller. So, I figured it must be the Mum. The only differences I could see between them and us were that they wore robes over their bodies. They had black hair as dark as space, with tiny glittery bits sprinkled over their locks. It made their hair look like stars in a midnight sky. The biggest difference was their skin. It was blue with green and purple splotches over it, like Ben's blue pyjamas with green monkeys and purple dinosaurs.

"Oh, I see," I said. "It's an easy mistake."

I didn't say, especially with my brother's dumb pyjamas, but I thought it. Then Merlin appeared at my feet and meowed.

"What's a crikey dickey?" Zek asked. "Is it a...." He pointed to a lower part of his body.

I could feel my face turning bright red. "It's a...er, well. Oh, never mind," I stammered, embarrassed.

"That's a clever Felis catus you have there," Deep-voice said.

My face cooled off, and I smiled for the first time.

"Yes, Merlin is," I said proudly.

"And you were brave coming to get your brother," Zek said.

My smile got bigger. "Thanks. Ben's a pain, but he's my pain," I muttered, feeling a little uncomfortable.

"Eybdoog," they said.

"No, wait. What about Ben? What will happen?" I asked.

"Nothing. He will walk back with you, but when Ben wakes up in the morning, he will not remember anything," Zek said.

"And me?" I asked.

"You will remember. But it is alright. No one will believe you. And I know you want to remember this," Deep-voice said.

"I do. I really do. And thank you. Thank you very much," I said.

"Come, Zek, and Dek," Deep-voice said.

"Will I see you again?" I asked. 

"Maybe," Zek answered.

Then the air shimmered, and they were gone. I took Ben's hand and followed Merlin home.

The next day, it was as if nothing had happened. Except Mum wanted to know why our slippers had twigs in them.

Ben had no idea, and I just shrugged. Then at breakfast, I kept staring at Ben, and when he became annoyed, I told him he would make a great robot. He seemed thrilled to hear it and ate the rest of his toast like a mechanical man.

Later that day, when I began to think I might have dreamt everything that had happened, I looked over at Merlin. He held me in his beautiful, strange eyes, and then he slowly, deliberately, closed his blue eye and winked.

"Yes, Merlin. Yes," I said, punching the air in delight, knowing it was true.

"Meow," he said.

This time, I'm sure Merlin smiled.

A.H. Syme is a prolific reader and writer of crime and speculative fiction. She spent many years teaching and enjoying the company of children. Writing this story allowed her the pleasure of remembering those children whose imaginations were gigantic, amazing, and wonderous. They shared their magic generously; she hopes the sparkles still shine.

The Sprites of Wimbledon Common
by Isabelle Johnson

If you walk through Wimbledon Common under the shadow of night,

You might find it strange; the world seems to change into a magical land of delight

The flowers bloom with ripe colours of green, the grass is woven from gold,

The leprechauns dance, the birds take their chance, but there's a story here never been told

If you look close in the shadows, glimpse in the dark, you may see a wing flutter by

Don't be scared, just be prepared for the critters that hide under night

For under the bushes and stems of flowers lurk fairies hidden from sight,

The smallest of creatures with the brightest of features called magical, whimsical sprites

Though tiny and charming, their smiles unalarming, make sure to keep a good space

Sprites love their own and will protect their home, if it means plucking the eyes from your face

If you happen to see this creature of glee, make sure to pay your respects

Bow lowly on knee, beneath their home tree, or your fingers they soon will collect

And before you leave, if you still don't believe, be wary of what follows you back

The sprites are quite proud, they'll follow in crowds, and surround you til the world goes black

But don't be frightened, the sprites are forgiving, unless you happen to be rude

Just be polite, leave after the night, or else you'll be utterly screwed

Next time you stop by Wimbledon Common and hear laughter ringing in the skies,

Admire the sound, but don't go around, for the sprites are plotting your demise

Isabelle Johnson is a 19-year-old author based in Memphis, TN. Her first book, *The Incredible Adventures of Mr. Marxadue*, was published in 2019, with the sequel to be released. Other works include, *The Curious Shop on Dandelion Lane* (2021), *A Place Called Time* (2022), *and I Can See the City* (2021). Along with books, Isabelle also has various works published with Crow's Feet Journal, Black Ink Fiction, Black Hare Press, and Raven and Drake Publishing.

Don't Dare go to Wimbledon Common at Night
by Lynne Phillips

Don't dare go to Wimbledon Common at night,

The creatures there will give you a terrible fright.

Some love to eat girls,

Dressed in ribbons and curls.

While other snaffle up boys,

And steal all their toys.

f course, it's always your choice,

But, listen to your inner voice.

Stay at home instead,

And snuggle up safe in bed.

Archie's mother closed the book and said, "Goodnight,

I hope that story doesn't keep you awake with fright."

Archie laughed at the idea and snuggled in bed,

Images from the story, running around in his head.

Wimbledon Common, he'd been there before.

Once with his Gran, on the way to the store.

There was grass, lots of trees, and a children's park.

But nothing scary, like those things in the dark.

A tapping at his window, a creaking of the door,

All the sounds Archie had heard before.

Nothing at all to be in despair,

And nothing to give a small boy a scare.

Eyes getting sleepy, and off to the land of dreams,

Where everything appears normal but is never as it seems.

A griffin appeared next to Archie's warm bed.

"Would you like an adventure?" the strange creature said.

Archie smiled with delight and climbed out of bed,

The images of the book still fresh in his head.

"You'll need your coat, scarf, slippers, and a warm hat.

It's cold outside, there's no doubt about that."

Archie sleepily replied, "That may be so,

But without my teddy, I don't want to go."

The griffin glared at the lad, but finally conceded,

Realising a compromise was certainly needed.

"The teddy can come but hurry up, lad.

The creatures are waiting, they're getting quite mad."

Archie donned some warm clothes and grabbed his wee bear,
And left his warm room with never a care.

He held on tight to the griffin, his heart all aquiver,
The cold air making his whole body shiver.

The moon was round and filled up the sky.
The man in the moon waved as they flew by.

The stars were all twinkling, so wonderfully bright.
Archie's eyes were wide open, in awe at the sight.

As the griffin dropped Archie hard on the ground,
The air was filled with a horrible sound.

Gnashing and clashing of creatures galore,
Filling the night with a terrible uproar.

Wimbledon Common

Archie rubbed his eyes, hoping to see

Where in the world he happened to be.

Surely not Wimbledon Common at night,

The place with the creatures that give you a fright?

A witch pulled on the tails of Archie's warm coat.

Her long, scrawny fingers snatched at his throat.

"Why are you not home in bed, my lad?

Are you here because you've been bad?"

Archie shrank from the witch. He shivered and shook.

His heart all a flutter from the old hag's stern look.

A dragon approached and said in a very loud roar,

"Be afraid, young man, of what we've in store.

Adventurous boys shouldn't come to the park,

Especially where creatures are out for a lark."

Next a giant crocodile came on the attack,

Forcing young Archie to take a step back.

Its jaws opened wide, and then closed with a snap.

The creatures all cheered and started to clap.

Archie pulled his coat tightly to ward off the cold.

Although scared inside, he tried to look bold.

His legs were atremble, and his head gave a shake.

He pinched himself to see if he was awake.

A goblin approached, his legs short and fat.

He rolled his eyes and said, "Fancy that.

A boy alone in the park, it should not be.

There are lots of scary things running free."

A fat, squat dwarf swung an enormous hoe

And almost chopped off Archie's big toe.

Wimbledon Common

Archie said, "The book was definitely right,
Wimbledon Common is scary at night."

An ugly troll stamped his feet and waved his giant fist.
"Let's get him. This young lad will never be missed.

Let's pull off his head and tear him apart.
I want first bite of his young heart."

A wolf licked his lips and looked at the lad,
His red eyes wide and definitely mad.

Archie hugged teddy, shook his fist, and said,
"You are just from a book my mother read,

For surely you all are not as you seem. 
I think you are part of a horrible dream.

I'll wake up in bed, and you won't be there.
There will only be me and my wee teddy bear."

The creatures all snarled and moved towards the boy.

"Didn't the book say we'd be after your toy?"

Now, Archie was scared of the creatures that night,

But he wasn't going to lose teddy without a good fight.

With one hand he hid teddy behind his small back,

Then turned to the creatures prepared for the attack.

The griffin swooped down, extending its claws,

And picked up young Archie, with never a pause.

"That's enough adventure, Archie," the griffin said.

"It's time I deposited you back in your bed."

Next morning, Archie awoke safe and snug in his bed,

Though the creatures from Wimbledon were still in his head.

He climbed out of bed and said to his teddy,

"I can smell bacon. I think breakfast is ready."

His mother said, "Archie, did you sleep well last night,

Or did reading that book keep you awake with fright?"

Archie gave a smile. "I slept soundly," he said.

Sometimes adventures should stay in your head.

Lynne Phillips' stories have been published by Zombie Pirate Publishing, Black Hare Press, Fantasia Divinity Publishing, Our Wonderful Anthology, and in various online magazines. She enjoys exploring the craft of writing stories and the challenge it presents. Her priority is spending time with her family while her passions are reading, writing, keeping fit and spending time at her farm. Connect with her on Facebook @lynne.phillips.505.

Miles Merk, Random, and the Dragon
by D.J. Elton

Every afternoon after school, it was Miles Merk's responsibility to walk Maxie, the family dog. Miles dreaded the chore. He thought Maxie was a smelly, yappy thing, and was sure Mum loved the pooch best—more than her own flesh and blood!

Miles would come home, and there, waiting at the front door in her pink pinny, was Mum, holding out Maxie's black plastic lead. She'd kiss him briskly on the top of his head, and say, "Good Boy." Miles was never certain whether she meant himself, or the dog.

On their walks, Maxie pulled Miles across the Common, such was the small creature's enthusiasm. Miles needed dragging as he didn't know how to enjoy the walk, his pet, the weather, or the funny sights one would see when ambling through the Common on a weekday afternoon. Every day they'd head along the outskirts of Wimbledon Common to Rushmere Pond, Maxie would sniff excitedly, pee, then run around in a circle.

This day was much like any other, though later than usual. Miles was grumpy. He just wanted to get to the Pond; avoid any bicycles, pedestrians, or larger dogs, and get home before dark. Mum was cooking his favourite—pizza with oodles of cheese—and his new book, The Dragon of Fitchmore Park, was waiting. But for once, Maxie was the one who needed prompting. He was lollygagging, shaking his lead, sniffing poles and going off the track. The sound of Maxie yapping, then throwing up, pulled Miles away from pizza and dragon-filled thoughts.

"Oh, you really are a bad dog," Miles grumbled, looking around to see if anyone was nearby. "I wish you were a dragon."

As he spoke, some odd things happened. The

streetlights started to flash brightly, and the group of gnarled trees Miles was walking beside seemed to grow taller, stretching until they stood erect. In the gloaming, their branches looked like spindly, outstretched hands. Miles decided he should hasten home, but a friendly sound stopped him in his tracks.

"Too late," said a strong female voice. Miles turned around and came face to face with a girl—a head taller than him, wearing a long, ice-blue coloured cape over a pair of old-fashioned breeches. Colours sparkled all around her. Her pale-green eyes were focussed on him, absorbing every detail.

"You want a dragon, then?" she said coolly.

Miles closed his mouth. It had been hanging open. He nodded keenly, unable to speak, nearly blinded by her shining. This isn't boring, he thought. In fact, it was turning into quite an adventure.

"I can change your dog into a dragon," she said matter-of-factly, "in return for you letting us stay at the bottom of your garden now and then."

Miles looked down at Maxie who was making a whining noise yet wagging his tail manically. That was encouraging.

Perhaps Maxie needed an adventure too?

"Deal?" she asked.

"Done deal." Miles said gleefully, feeling very pleased with himself. His very own dragon. He could fly to Turkey. Or Australia. Or South America.

"Size?" she asked. "And colour?"

Miles was quick. The boy knew his dragons.

"As big as our garage. And green." He thought a green dragon would fit in most places and not cause too much unnecessary attention.

"All done. See you in the garden with my friends here." She indicated towards the group of trees. "My name's Random."

Maxie had grown exponentially. He still had the same droopy spaniel eyes, but now there was fire in them. He looked furtively at Miles, and when they both looked behind, Random had disappeared.

"Cor! A faerie!" Miles was excited, hopping from one foot to the other.

🦋 🦋 🦋

Miles wasn't sure how to proceed. Maxie was still

increasing in size. He felt glaringly obvious standing on Wimbledon Common next to a large green dragon with little gold knobs around its head and tail. They needed to get home quickly, before anyone saw the new Maxie and called the police, zoo, fire brigade, or even the lost dogs' home. It was getting darker, and he was ravenously hungry.

"Let's go home for dinner then." said the dragon, as if reading Miles' mind. "Hop on." Twisting his small lizard-like head towards the boy, Maxie moved closer. Miles, feeling somewhere between astonished and overwhelmed, did as he was told, grabbing onto several little shiny bumps on the beast's back. As he clutched onto the dragon's neck for dear life, they ascended over the lake, flying in a circle above the Common. It was going to be easy, he reassured himself. Miles nestled between its neck ridges on the dragon's neck. It did smell a bit like Maxie, but more dragon really. Miles was feeling safe flying high above the houses dotted below. He could even see his home and Mum's car wasn't there. Maybe she'd popped up to the shop? He hoped she hadn't gone out looking for him and Maxie. Mum loved Maxie much more than Miles ever had. Before Miles could agonise over Mum's likely response to Maxie going missing, they were ready to land, Maxie's dragon tail uprooting a few small trees. It was going to be a bit awkward, but Miles was so thrilled to actually have a real pet dragon that he wasn't thinking too much about future planning.

They had landed in the backyard near the wide-open garage. Miles slid bumpety bump down the dragon's back, as it crept into the garage, a bit like Maxie used to, looking for his basket. Except it now squashed itself beneath the roof and the tip of its tail, like a sharp arrow, stuck out underneath. Miles blinked. Who would believe it? A dragon in your backyard? Where was Mum?

It was dark now, but the house lights were on. Miles found an old crate to stand on from the garage to climb through the open kitchen window as he didn't have a front door key.

Mum had cooked up a storm. Three large trays of cheesy topped pizza—his favourite —stood proudly on the kitchen table. Gosh, he thought, so much pizza. Mum had been really busy. Smelling the freshly baked treat, mouth-watering, he couldn't wait to eat it. But it was not to be.

A huge whoosh of heat, flames, and dragon breath flew through the window. In two noisy, slurpy licks, Maxie had poked his lizard head inside and demolished all three trays of pizza.

"Stop it." Miles was nearly crying. "You'll burn the house down." For a few seconds, the creature's head was stuck as he frantically tried to withdraw it, and melted cheese was dripping from his slobbery dragon lips. Miles could hear a car pulling up outside the house. Oh no, Mum!

"Get in the garage. Quickly," he hissed at the dragon. "Stay there until I come and get you. Bad dragon." Miles slammed the garage door, and practically dove into the kitchen, sustaining a small bump as his head hit the dining table. Standing up, feeling wonky, he came face to face with Mum holding two bags of groceries.

"Where have you been?" Mum asked, puzzled.

Good, she's not angry, thought Miles. "Walking Maxie," he said as he stood in front of the oven trying to hide the empty pizza trays.

"Where's Maxie?" said Mum, on a roll of interrogation. She put the shopping down on the bench then started sniffing the air, pulling a face. Miles wondered what to say. He couldn't lie to Mum, but he knew he couldn't tell her about the dragon, the faerie, and the talking trees.

"What's that smell?" said Mum, starting to walk towards Miles.

Mum shrieked loudly. Miles jumped.

"Where's the pizza?"

Miles shrugged. What could he say? Dragon smoke? A dragon ate our pizza.

Miles looked blank. "I'll wash up," he said and sprinted to the table, collecting the three trays, and placing them in the sink. He fully pulled on both taps, squirting detergent and trying to look helpful.

"Where is it? Did you eat all of it, Miles?" She looked baffled. "Tell me."

This is too hard, thought Miles. Then a bright idea came, not really a lie.

"Maxie ate it." Well, it was sort of true. Mum couldn't accuse him of telling lies.

🐾 🐾 🐾

After a quick dinner of cheese and tomato toasties, Mum sent Miles to bed, warning him they would talk more about it in the morning. Mum didn't ask again about the dog. She must have thought Maxie was in the garage. Miles didn't sleep well that night. In fact, he woke up for the third time at 4 a.m. and decided to go down and check on the dragon. Pulling on his thick dressing gown, he crept quietly down the stairs, careful not to wake Mum, and snuck out to the direction of the garage.

"Oi. Down here," said a voice.

Miles looked around. A branch poked him in the belly—it was a walking, talking tree which he'd forgotten about, being more absorbed in the dragon adventure.

"Oi. Boy. Miles. Here." It was the faerie, Random. He heard the dragon snoring loudly and thought it better to go down to the bottom of the garden. She was standing near an outdoor chair, hovering over it. Miles could see she was above ground with sparkles flying all around her, pink, cream, and purple ones. It was fascinating.

"You need to control your dragon," said Random. "It may do some damage. We don't want that." Miles sat down on a rock and watched the trees move, dancing each time Random spoke.

"How to do that?" he asked. "I've never had a dragon before."

"I could make him invisible," she said. "So he doesn't get

you into a lot of trouble.”

“Yes, please. Do that.” Miles nodded his head frantically. “I want to keep him. I do. Really.” Random rolled her eyes and muttered some whispery words, and there was a change in the atmosphere.

“We’re very pleased to be staying at the bottom of your garden,” said Random. “It’s nice here. Peaceful and fresh.”

“You’re welcome.” Miles grinned. “What about Mum? She’ll be missing Maxie. And how do I explain the missing pizza? At least I won’t need to mention the dragon now.”

“I know you don’t want to tell lies to your Mum,” said Random. “What about this idea? Tell her Maxie ate the pizza and that Maxie vanished. You don’t have to tell her when it happened. She’ll be sad about Maxie, but later today a new dog, just like Maxie, will arrive. A gift for your Mum.” Random beamed at him, a triple glow with sparkling colours flying around her head as she spoke. “What do you think, Miles?”

What could he say? It sounded like a foolproof plan.

It worked.

Mum was so happy, she made pizza the next night. The new dog was cute, and Mum called her Molly. It was love at first sight.

Random liked life at the bottom of the garden. She and Miles often had breakfast together amongst the flowers and bushes, discussing the many ways to keep pet dragons happy.

And if you were to keep a keen eye, at certain times of the night, you would see a green and gold dragon with a boy on its back flying over Wimbledon Common.

D.J. Elton is a poet and speculative fiction writer living in the Blue Mountains of Sydney. Her work has been published with Black Hare Press, Clarendon House Books, Deadset Press, Barrio Blues Press, and more. She likes being in the country, meditation, and connecting with family.

When Darkness Falls
by J.W. Garrett

When darkness falls, that's when the Common comes alive,

Stars burst from their cages; the fog rises…

Like clockwork, the ritual dance begins;

With a rush of activity, breath heaving, all on the prowl till evening ends.

Hidden from humans, the creatures crawl from places unknown,

Loose at last, through the murkiness they roam.

Bold in the gloom of night, they claim the waterways and woodlands once again;

Time ticks down till sunrise will swallow them and win.

Until then the wind whispers and floats over the bog,

The marshes alive with animals scuttling and skittering along.

Vampire bunnies sniff out their prey.

The fae set their traps in the thorns, catching whatever comes their way.

Worms with sharp teeth, bursting with colour, glow with tiny pinpoints of light,

Changing shade with the meals they rip apart and consume with delight.

Above, swishing across the inky blackness, dragons take to the sky,

Their wings slice the air, pumping hard; all the creatures know why.

Their treasure is near, the vibration ringing louder and louder as the night drones on—

Thumpidy, thump, thump, thump, it beats, till all glance upward willing them gone.

Their hearts pound in unison like the chorus of a song.

Then swoop, the downdraft of wings, a ribbon of flame…the wait is so long,

While each one tracks the circling beasts, wondering is it me?

They gather, trembling for those who may meet their destiny;

Jaws yawn open; moments stop while the wind spews a low hiss.

Then night surrenders with the first peek of orange, and the creatures retreat into the mist.

Till the evening rises over the bog tonight again, peace—they sleep;

Safe for now from the eerie rhythm while they tunnel down deep.

J.W. Garrett is a multi-award-winning author. Initiated into fantasy after reading *The Hobbit* in elementary school, she has been hooked ever since. She writes speculative fiction from the sunny beaches of Jacksonville, Florida, but loves the mountains of Virginia where she was born. Her writings include novels, short stories, and poetry. *Remeon's Legacy*, the final book in her fantasy series, Realms of Chaos, is out now. When she's not hanging out with her characters, her favourite activities are reading, running and spending time with family. www.jwgarrett.com.

A Carnival at Wimbledon Common
by Jodie Angell

Marnie took a large mouthful of the pink, fluffy cotton candy. Her eyes gleamed with delight.

Her best friend, Sophie, skipped beside her. Their parents lingered close by, keeping a watchful eye on them.

Bright, florescent lights sparkled in the trees, and multicoloured bunting hung from post to post. The Ferris wheel spun, and laughter echoed across Wimbledon Common. The carnival had arrived, and the production began.

Dancers on stilts twirled in front of Marnie and Sophie. A man in a pinstripe suit gave a theatrical bow, grinned, then strode off through the crowd.

They held hands as they scarfed their candy and skipped toward the theater by the lake.

Thick red velvet curtains were drawn, and a circular spotlight lit the centre of the stage. Children and parents took their seats in the wooden chairs while a hawker walked down the aisle selling portions of popcorn.

"Popcorn for three pounds. Salty and sweet. Get ready for the show!" she chimed.

Rachel, Marnie's mother, waved her over and handed the woman the coins. With a gentle smile on her face, she passed the popcorn to her daughter.

Sophie scooted closer to her friend, then shoved her hand into the bag. "I can't wait for the production."

"Do you think it'll be scary?" Marnie held her hand halfway to her mouth. The sweet scent of her snack filled her nostrils. Her eyes widened.

"There's nothing to fear, my dear," Rachel said. "The ticket sellers assured me the show was suitable for children."

Although her words were filled with conviction, she eyed

Sophie's mother, Julie, cautiously.

Julie shrugged before tucking into the popcorn.

The friends leaned back into their chairs with ease as the music began and the drapes were pulled aside. A set was revealed—large wooden cut-out trees and hills, and a midnight blue backdrop with a full moon dangling from the top of the structure.

Smoke billowed across the wooden floor and howling wolves sounded from the speakers on either side of the stage.

Marnie drew her knees to her chest and leaned forward in excitement. The lights dimmed.

A narrator dressed in back took her position on the left side. The spotlight shifted its focus to her.

"Many years ago, there lived a middle-aged man by the name of Fred Draper. He had a quiet life in the mountains of the Northern Lakes. But all was not as it seems." As the words left her mouth, an actor dressed in overalls came onto the stage. He rested a gun prop against his shoulder and scoured the trees.

Marnie tugged on her mother's sleeves. "I don't like guns."

"It's not real, honey." She patted her, gently.

"Darn monsters, where are ye?" Fred called. "Eatin' all me cattle and sheep. Ye nice pelts will look good on me floorboards."

Julie glanced at Rachel from the corner of her eyes, and mouthed, "Talking about killing animals?"

Rachel laughed. "They're monsters."

The actor shot various monsters who crept out from behind the trees. Ones with horns, razor-sharp teeth, and piercing red eyes.

The monsters fell to the floor, and blood spilled onto the wooden floor. Fred blew the plumes of smoke that rose from his gun barrel, then retired to his cottage.

When he was alone, another dark monster climbed the hill, howled at the moon, then dashed into the forest.

"The Shadow evaded Fred's attempts to kill him. He stayed hidden in the trees, feasting on elk and birds. But several years passed, and the Shadow no longer enjoyed the restrictions of his home within the forest," the narrator said.

The monster stalked onto the stage. His harrowing gaze landed on Marnie, who squealed and pulled her mother's arm over her face.

The Shadow jumped into the crowd, stalked up the aisle between the seated spectators. He stared at children, bared his teeth, then growled. Once he arrived at the row in which Marnie and Sophie sat, he turned toward them, weaving his way through the row.

He stopped in front of the girls. Marnie's heart pounded and her eyes glistened. She quivered next to her mother.

The monster leaned closer, sniffed her, bared his teeth once more before he scurried out of the aisle.

A deep sigh escaped her mouth as the Shadow grew further away from her. He continued to sniff children amongst the crowd until he finally chose his victim—a small boy with brown hair.

He took the boy in his arms, threw him over his shoulder. The boy screamed as he was hauled onto the stage. The audience remained silent, unable to remove their gaze from the play.

The monster brought him two tusks attached to a headband. "You," he grunted. "Monster."

The boy shook as he placed the object on his head.

"The Shadow grew tired of being the last monster, and so, decided to create an initiation for lost children," the narrator said, and the spotlight flicked to her. "He made it his mission to kidnap children to join his clan of new-world monsters. Feral children."

Child actors crawled into the spotlight from either side, exposing their teeth, and growling at the boy from the audience. Each of them wore antlers, and thick lines of white paint streaked their faces.

They howled loudly, piercing the silent night. Fred, roused from his cottage, blundered onto the stage, waving his gun. He stood, frozen in place, and his mouth opened as he stared at the swarm of monsters ahead of him.

The Shadow crept forward until he squared up to the farmer. The Shadow pushed his shoulders back and wrinkled his nose. Fred retreated, his eyes darted from one feral child to the next.

"The feral children lived in the woods with the Shadow, luring in other children, while Fred kept his distance," the narrator said. "The monsters' clan grew larger, and he was outnumbered. One night, they came for him."

The tribe, now fifteen monsters strong, beat their fists against their chest, and charged at Fred, tackling him to the floor. His screams filled the air as he was dragged

backstage—a trail of his blood smeared across the wooden floorboards.

The audience erupted into applause. Marnie and Sophie exchanged horrified glances.

"M-mummy," Marnie said, her bottom lip quivering. "M-monsters are s-scary."

"Oh, you'll be all right, dear, it's only a play." Her mother smoothed her hair, gently. "Come on. Let's get some food."

They walked toward the main route that weaved through the various stalls and performances across Wimbledon Common.

Ahead of them was a florescent, decorated stall, and on its shelves were a variety of monsters for sale.

"Teddies for ten pounds," the salesman called.

Families gathered around, choosing which one to buy, while Marnie cast a cautious glance at the stall. She shivered, and the hairs on her neck stood on end.

A clown blundered past, blaring a horn, and startling the girls. They squealed and stumbled back into their mothers.

"Looks like there is another performance that way." Rachel pointed in the clown's direction.

The girls held hands, and their mothers followed behind.

The crowd formed a crescent moon around the performers.

A woman dressed in a red leotard blew fire from her mouth, encouraging applause from the crowd. One man swallowed a sword, while another juggled fire-lit batons. Smoke plumed across Wimbledon Common.

Marnie tugged Sophie closer, weaving through the crowd until they stood at the front. Her gaze locked with the clown's. His lips curled into a maniacal grin, and he tilted his head to the side.

She clamped her hands over her eyes as her mother drew her closer. "I don't like clowns."

"It's all right, dear."

A purple tinge to the sky indicated evening, and the performances grew wilder. Groans and moans echoed from the right of the crowd. Spectators turned away from the acts following the noise.

Rachel glanced at Julie. "Did you know there was another act booked this late?"

"Perhaps a surprise?"

Sophie trembled, squeezing her friend's hand tightly.

They reached the crowd right as screams pierced the air. People stumbled backward. Marnie yelped, clinging to her mother's waist.

A horde of zombies lumbered across the grass. Black liquid oozed from holes in their bodies, skin peeled back from their faces, and their eyes were bloodshot.

A siren blared, and more zombies gathered, circling the crowd. They edged closer, shrinking the space between them. The spectators huddled together, unable to locate a way out.

A zombie grabbed Marnie by the arm, pulling her into the horde. She wailed as she was lifted into the air and carried above their heads.

Applause filled her ears, and she frowned. Why would they cheer monsters who wanted to kill her?

Marnie was plonked onto the ground at the other side of the horde. Someone handed her a gift bag filled with teddies and sweets. "We hope you had a lovely time! Will we be seeing you again next year?"

Her lip quivered and her heart pounded.

She shook her head.

Jodie Angell grew up in South Wales, UK. She started writing at the age of eleven, entering children's anthologies. Her first book, *Crimson Kiss*, is signed with Champagne Book Group. Jodie explores all genres. She has recently expanded her repertoire and has signed several dark short stories with Black Hare Press. Twitter: @JodieA_Author.

The Hoblots Under the Windmill
by Stephen Johnson

I travelled by Wimbledon Common one bright and sunny day

Under the Windmill for a quick bite to enjoy my stay

When from behind me I heard a great and mighty growl

And along with it, a smell that came off old and foul

I turned to see with astonished eyes

A creature staring back at me full of surprise

"Who are you?" I exclaimed with a bit of fear

Regally, it replied, "I am the Watcher of the Windmill my

dear"

My name is Sir Marcus, and I watch over this place"

I looked back at this creature with a curious face

"But dear sir, you look like a dragon to me"

"Au contraire my friend, I am a Grand Hoblot, you see

My kind have watched over the Common for ages

For so long as it has been written in the Hoblot pages

Only the truly good gain the honour of seeing us during the

day

And only with a swift breeze that blows the Windmill you

may

Catch a glimpse of us Hoblots as we stand

Guarding our precious Windmill and the Common land

Please sit and listen a while as I tell you a tale

About the Hoblots who live here, in grand detail

Hoblots are noble creatures, true and devoted to the core

A long and distinguished history of ancient lore

For though I look as a dragon to you now

Hoblots change shapes and colours, for tomorrow I could be

a cow

Our special talents help us to hide

In case there is ever a time that should abide

Wimbledon Common

Where we are needed to help anyone in despair

Someone in the Common who may need our care

For in that time, you can count on one of us

To help and aid in any way without any fuss

We make the Windmill our home but out of sight

Rarely we travel out during the day or the light

But I sensed your goodness as you passed by

Us Hoblots can sense those who cause trouble or lie

For the special people that a Hoblot does friend

Truly have a bond without ever an end

With that introduction, I invite you to see

The Hoblot land within the Wimbledon as it normally be

Beneath this dear Mill lie my family and kin

A humble and cosy abode, this thing we call our Den

The last of our kind dwell here in this space

But I caution anyone who sees a Hoblot face

Tricks we play as we change our forms and shape

We rarely are recognised in public, always a means of escape

I introduce you to the last three Hoblots of the Mill

To my right is Sir Thomas, please if you would kneel

For he is our leader and noblest of all

To my left is Sir Anthony, his bravery at your call

And for the third Hoblot, you have already met

For it is I, which you have most likely bet

My dear lad, I humbly request your name

Who is this person now of such goodness and fame?"

Blushing, I looked at Sir Marcus and with a grin

I spoke through humble lips, quiet and thin

"My name is Stephen, and it is an honour to meet you

But I beg to know why of the Hoblots there are so few?"

He looked back at me with a fatherly wink

"Oh, my friend, at a time there were a few more I think

But over the years the land has changed so much

The people who visit no longer care or are out of touch

We live for the goodness in the people who come through

For so long we waited for someone so true

When today you appeared suddenly to stop at our door

We humbly invite you to grace our floor

Please know you are welcome in our home day or night

The Windmill will always stand as a beacon and towering

light

And with that, my story will come to an end

But fear not, Mr Stephen, for now we are dear friends

Venture out now again past the Common, but before you go

Know that we Hoblots will always know

Your gracious friendship has rekindled our hope

In the goodness that exists outside of our scope."

With a wave I travelled back out towards the city of men

Wondering if I ever would see my friends the Hoblots again

But each time I venture on a walk through the park

I often stop at the Windmill hoping for a spark

Of a quick breeze to alert my friends I am near

In hopes to say hello to the Hoblots I hold so dear.

Stephen Johnson is a retired Naval Officer, husband, father, and Chihuahua dad serving 22 years on four different ships over his career. Jumpmaster Press will publish his first novel, *The Fizz Prophecy*, in 2023. His novellas of the *Tales of Terror from the Bluff City* are available on Amazon, *The Deal With Madame Marguerite* (Episode One) and *Let the Good Times Roll* (Episode Two). His short stories appear in anthologies from Scare Street's *Night Terrors*, Volumes 8 and 17, No Bad Books' Released, Breaking Rules Europe's *Death Ship*, and Ink'd Publishing *Hidden Villains* Anthology. He can be found on Instagram @sejmsu.

I Don't Believe in Goblins
by Lynne Phillips

There was a little girl, who had a little curl,

Right in the middle of her forehead.

When she was good, she was very, very good,

But when she was bad, she was horrid.

—Henry Wadsworth Longfellow, "There Was a Little Girl"

Roxanne Jennings, aged eight, lived with her mother, father, three-year-old brother Max, and older sister Bella. Max and Bella were dark-haired and brown-eyed, like their father. Roxanne had blonde, curly hair, blue eyes, and an angelic face like her mother—

but looks can be deceiving. At times, Mrs Jennings wondered how one little girl could be so naughty, yet at other times be so kind and thoughtful.

Snatching the toy car from Max's hands, Roxanne held it above his head. She laughed as he cried and tried to reach for it.

"Stop teasing your brother, Roxanne," Mrs Jennings said. "Say you're sorry. Give him back his car and go outside to play."

Roxanne smiled sweetly. "Sorry Max." She placed the car in his hands. "Broom, broom," she said as Max's small hands clutched the car.

"Broom, broom," he echoed as he pushed it across the floor.

Bella lay on the sofa, ear buds firmly in her ears, her fingers tapping the beat as she listened to her favourite music. Roxanne couldn't resist the temptation. She pulled the earbuds out and threw them on the table. Red-faced, Bella sprang up and chased her sister.

"Roxanne, late at night when the moon disappears behind a cloud, goblins come out and take away naughty children. You'd better be careful. If you keep on being horrible, you'll be next," Bella threatened.

"I don't believe in goblins," Roxanne declared, poked out her tongue and raced out the door.

Chester, the family's cat, sat cleaning himself on the windowsill. Roxanne pulled his tail as she walked past. "Meow," Chester wailed.

"Leave the cat alone," Mrs Jennings yelled.

Roxanne picked up Chester and patted him. "I'm sorry, Chester," she whispered.

At dinner, Roxanne was on her best behaviour. Bathed and dressed in her pyjamas, her golden ringlets tied back from her face, it was hard for Mrs Jennings to believe it was the same child. After dinner, Roxanne offered to dry the dishes and read a bedtime story to Max.

"She can be really sweet," Mrs Jennings told her husband after Roxanne went to bed. "I don't understand where the naughtiness comes from."

"She's the middle child. Often, they feel left out. Maybe she does it for attention?" Mr Jennings suggested.

"Perhaps, but I think it's more than that."

At school the next day, Roxanne pushed a boy over, shouted at her best friend, and refused to do her schoolwork.

"Roxanne Jennings, I think it's time I spoke to your parents," Miss Robinson said.

Mr and Mrs Jennings apologised to the teacher for their daughter's behaviour.

"Is she naughty all the time?" Mrs Jennings asked.

"No, that's what I don't understand. At times, she can be the kindest, most thoughtful child in the class," Miss Robinson replied. "Last week she helped a kindergarten child who had fallen over and put a bandage on his knee. Yesterday she offered to tidy the classroom."

"We'll talk to her," Mr Robinson said. "If you can think of a reason for her bad behaviour, please let us know."

Over the next week, there were times when Roxanne was helpful. She took the dog for a walk, carried the groceries from the car, put away her clothes, and tidied her room, but she also chased the chickens until they were too exhausted to lay eggs, walked muddy feet through the house, and yelled at her mother when told she had to clean it up.

Bella rolled her eyes at her little sister. "Roxanne, you'd better keep an eye on the moon because, one night, when the dark clouds cover it, the goblins will be on the lookout for horrible children. There are times when you are definitely horrid."

"I don't believe in goblins. They're not real, so they can't come and take me away," Roxanne retorted then went outside to help her dad in the garden.

"This naughtiness has to stop, Roxanne," he said. "You know we all love you. You don't have to be horrible to get our attention."

"I don't know why I'm bad. It's like I have no control over it. I'd rather be good."

He gave her a hug. "Come on, let's wash our hands. It's time for dinner."

That night, the moon hid behind dark grey clouds. Asleep in her bed, Roxanne didn't hear the goblin tapping on the window, but she did dream something carried her away into the night and she couldn't find her way back home.

She woke with a start, her heart racing. She pinched herself to make sure she was awake.

I'm glad I was only dreaming. That was very scary.

She looked over at the other bed. Bella slept soundly.

Bella was mean to say goblins would get me. It made have a nightmare. Luckily, I don't believe in goblins.

Roxanne went back to sleep. The goblin tapped louder, but neither Roxanne nor Bella heard him.

⚊ ⚊ ⚊

For a few weeks, Roxanne was on her best behaviour. With her golden locks tied back off her face with a ribbon, she played hopscotch with her best friend and did all her schoolwork. She kept her side of the room tidy and didn't annoy Bella. And she took Rusty, the dog, for a walk to the park.

On Friday, Bella was excited. She was going to a dance; her first one. Mrs Jennings had sewn a beautiful dress for her to wear. Twirling around in it, Bella laughed. "This is a beautiful dress, Mum. Thank you. I am so excited."

Knowing Bella was sweet on a boy in her class, Roxanne

tried not say anything, but, as a curl fell down on her forehead, she blurted out, "Bella, Bella, dressed in yella', going to the dance to kiss her fella'."

Bella blushed. "I am not, Roxie. I don't even like anyone special. You're just being mean because you're not invited."

"What about Charlie?" Roxanne teased.

Bella started to cry.

Mrs Jennings' face was angry. "I won't have you spoiling Bella's first dance, Roxanne. Go to your room. Don't be naughty."

Roxanne stomped off.

"Come on Bella, dry your eyes. Forget about Roxanne. Have a great time at the dance. Dad will take you and Lucy to the dance, and Lucy's father will bring you home."

In the car, Mr Jennings overheard Bella telling Lucy how unkind Roxanne had been.

"I hope the moon disappears behind the clouds tonight and the goblins take her away. I'm sick of her being horrid."

👺 👺 👺

The dance was a great success. Bella had two dances with Charlie.

Roxanne was snoring softly when Bella climbed into bed and fell asleep. They were both in a deep sleep when the dark clouds raced across the sky and covered the moon.

A goblin tapped on the window. Nobody heard him, so he tapped louder. Roxanne woke up, rubbed her eyes, and looked around. The window was sliding open and a funny little man, only as tall as Max, was climbing into the room.

"Bella, wake up. Someone is climbing in through the window. I think it might be a goblin," Roxanne whispered.

Bella said sleepily, "Don't be silly. I only made that up to stop you from being mean. Go back to sleep." She rolled over and was soon fast asleep again.

The room was dark. Roxanne couldn't see clearly.

A voice said, "Marigold, the queen of the goblins, has ordered me to take you to our kingdom in Wimbledon Common. She wishes to speak to you about your behaviour."

"I don't believe in goblins," Roxanne said.

"That maybe so, but it doesn't mean we don't exist."

"Are you a goblin?"

"Of course. My name is Prince Gumboldie. Now you must come with me. Mother will be waiting."

He grabbed Roxanne's hand. The room began to spin, and she was lifted out of bed and flying out the window.

"Help, Bella," she cried, but it was too late. She was being pulled through the darkness away from her house. Her heart was beating so fast, she thought it would burst out of her chest. There were lots of strange noises—an owl's hoot, the plaintive cry of a fox, and other sounds Roxanne couldn't identify—and the night was so black, she could only see dark shapes and shadows.

She knew where Wimbledon Common was. She'd been there before with her family for a picnic. The Common was very big, with lots of trees. She and Bella had climbed one and played hide-and-seek. It was fun during the day, but she'd never been there at night. She didn't know what to expect.

Far below in the distance, through the inky night, Roxanne spied a bright light.

"Is that where we are going?" she asked the prince, but he didn't answer.

Roxanne felt herself falling. Prince Gumboldie dropped her on the ground next to a huge bonfire. It flickered and crackled, its bright flame rising high into the sky.

Around the fire's edge, Roxanne could see lots of scary faces as the flames flickered. None of them were smiling; they all glared at her. One pulled her hair. Another kicked her in the shins, and a third punched her arm.

"Ouch!" Roxanne cried. "Don't be horrible."

Somewhere from the darkness, a voice declared, "Miss Roxanne, you have been summoned to my court because you are being mean and horrid yourself." A lady stepped into the light. She adjusted the crown on her head, the jewels sparkling in the firelight.

"I am Esmerelda, queen of the Goblins."

Roxanne felt she should curtsy, but her knees were shaking so much, she only managed a small bow.

The queen continued, "Being horrible and nasty is what goblins do best. We are not happy you are trying to be better at it than we are."

"But I don't really want to be horrid," Roxanne replied. "I don't know why I am. I don't seem to be able to control my behaviour."

The queen turned, her eyes seeking someone.

"What do you think, Granny Gollygosh?" she asked.

A little old lady stepped forward and looked Roxanne up

and down, before saying, with a smile, "The answer is clear. The curl on your forehead is the problem, my dear."

She pulled a large pair of scissors out of her pocket, snipped off the golden curl, and threw it into the fire, where it sizzled and burned.

"Do you think that will help me be good?" Roxanne asked.

Granny Gollygosh touched the end of her nose. "That depends on whether you believe in goblins, and whether you are willing to leave all mischief and horrible things for us to enjoy."

Roxanne looked around at the ring of goblins. How could she not believe they were real? "I believe in goblins," she said.

The goblins clapped and cheered. The fire disappeared, along with all the goblins. Roxanne found herself on her own in the dark.

"How will I get home?" she wailed; it was her nightmare coming true.

Out of the gloom, the queen's voice said, "Close your eyes and wish you were back in your bed."

Roxanne closed her eyes tightly and wished. When she

opened them, she was safe in her bed, and Bella was still asleep.

The next day, Roxanne thought it was all a dream, but when she looked in the mirror, the curl was missing from the middle of her forehead.

From that day on, whenever her curls grew long, Roxanne tied them back with a bow. She was occasionally naughty, but she was never horrid again; she left that for the goblins.

Lynne Phillips' stories have been published by Zombie Pirate Publishing, Black Hare Press, Fantasia Divinity Publishing, Our Wonderful Anthology, and in various online magazines. She enjoys exploring the craft of writing stories and the challenge it presents. Her priority is spending time with her family while her passions are reading, writing, keeping fit and spending time at her farm. Connect with her on Facebook @lynne.phillips.505.

The Disgraced Jujuboo
by Dawn Burdett

"Joobee!" Jayby whispered urgently. "What *are* you doing!"

Joobee startled for a moment and then grinned, the huge conker held aloft as he looked down on his intended target below. "What?" he asked with a shrug. "It's fun and it does no harm."

He dropped the nut on the sleeping child—one of the "talls"—below, his laugh tinkling when the boy sprang up in fright and ran away, hands held to his head.

"Joobee! We are *supposed* to be invisible to humankind. We are *supposed* to be silent, We are *supposed* to only be felt on the breeze. We are *supposed* to be the shadow just caught in the corner of their eyes. We are *not* supposed to stand in trees chucking acorns at them!" Jayby said, crossly, her voice rising in tempo and her cheeks pinking.

"Supposed, supposed, *supposed*," Joobee mimicked, then added, "Conker."

"What?"

"Conker…it's a conker. Not an acorn."

"Same difference."

Joobee raised his eyebrows, the sleeping caterpillars above his eyes rippling with agitation. "They are *quite* different, Jayby, as you would know if you didn't sleep in bot-sci class."

The sparrow nesting in Jayby's dishevelled hair poked it's head out for a moment, sensing drama.

"I wasn't asleep!" Jaybe said, flushing down to her bellybutton. I was thinking about our magical herbs assignment that's due tomorrow.

"Assignment!? Your eyes were closed, you were snoring loud enough to wake the Cerne Abbas Giant, and drool was puddling on the table beneath your face—your sparrows were bathing in it!"

"Were not," Jayby retorted.

"Fruit and seed."

"Uh?"

"Acorns and conkers. Fruits and seeds—that's how they're different."

"Oh," Jayby said, forgetting what she was admonishing Joobee for.

She straightened down her black frock coat and muttered, "We should get back, we're late—everyone'll wonder where we got to."

"Race ya!" Joobee yelled as took a flying leap off the bough he was standing on, caught hold of a leafless branch, then swung (doing Tarzan screams—*ahh-aahAhhhhh-AhhAhhAaaahhhhhh*-ing—all through the woods as he went) to the next tree. "C'mon!' he called once he'd landed almost at the top of the tree.

"Invisible. Silent. Shadows…" Jayby grumbled, making her way down to the Common floor as quickly and quietly as she could.

But when they got back to the Jujuboo tree—their kinsfolk's large house pods disguised as bird's nests—their people were juddering about in consternation, so much so, that the tree was aquiver.

Down below, one of the talls was leaning his ladder against the trunk, clearly ready to climb. "It's up here, mate! Sure I seen one of them land in this 'ere tree."

"What's going on?" Joobee whispered, his bravado evaporating.

"I don't know," Jayby said, her brow furrowed.

The queen of Jujubee, Jainty, landed on the branch next to them. "We need to find a new home," she said in a serious tone.

Joobee paled. "But why? We love it here."

"It seems *someone*"—she peered closely at Joobee—"may not have been as discrete as they should have been…"

Joobee gulped. Jayby smirked.

"Would you two know anything about this?" Queen Jainty asked, one tiny butterfly brow raised.

"Nu- Uh… Uhm—" stuttered Joobee.

"You see what you've done!" Jayby blurted out. "All that messing about, dropping *conkers* on people. You thought it was such fun, but now we have to leave!"

"Joobee! Is this true? You forsook all our laws for 'fun'?"

Queen Jainty gasped, her eyes widening. "Your fun has caused us to lose our home. Your fun has meant we have to hide from humankind. Was your fun worth all that?"

Joobee hung his head in shame, trying not to cry, and went off to help pack.

Later, as they bounced off the tree branches, in search of a new home (silently, invisibly, like a small breeze), they all looked back longingly at the home they could never return to.

৬ ৬ ৬

To this day, no one knows where the Common's Jujuboo colony now resides. Mainly thanks to Joobee and his acor— I mean conkers.

Between writing, working, and designing book covers, **Dawn Burdett** manages to get some sleep…at least, that's the plan. www.dawnburdett.com.

A Bargain of Shadows
by Leanbh Pearson

This story is about bargaining with shadows, my brother's bravery and my quest to reunite us. My brother, Edward, was kind and selfless, but I was sickly, always confined to my bed with mystery illnesses the doctors could not cure. As we left childhood behind, I grew sicker and Edward more desperate to save me from the looming spectre of death. We both knew never to go into Wimbledon Common, rumours of the forest within where magical beings lived, where the otherworldly and mortal realm met. Determined to heal me, Edward left my side one night, venturing onto the Common—a meadow and forest owned by none, wedged between housing estates—a place

of wildest magic.

I felt the moment Edward made his bargain with the sorcerer. My lungs cleared, the fever lifted, and I felt stronger than I ever had before. I was as well as any child. But when Edward returned later that night, he no longer had a shadow.

"What happened to your shadow?" I asked, leaping from the bed to hug him.

"It doesn't matter if you are well. Are you recovered, Emily?" he asked.

I grinned. "I feel like I could fly."

Edward hugged me, and if he felt any ill-effects from not having a shadow, he did not show them.

"Don't you miss your shadow?" I asked him one evening.

"No. Without you, Emily, I would never be whole—but I can spare my shadow."

Weeks passed, and my health continued to improve. It overjoyed our parents at first. But soon many of the neighbours whispered about my strange recovery and the absence of Edward's shadow. Many accused Edward of sorcery, whispering that he must have exchanged his shadow for terrible powers. None of it was true, but the gossip and glances followed him everywhere. Even our parents watched Edward with undisguised wariness. And it was when we both saw those same tendencies in our parents that Edward packed his bags one night and quietly disappeared.

When I woke the next morning, Edward was gone. Knowing where he would go, I followed him onto Wimbledon Common and into those dark and tangled woods. But the forest guardians had other ideas, the trees trying to block my path, twiggy hands catching my hair and clothing as I crossed the invisible border between our mortal realm and the Otherworld.

The forest was strange and full of unfamiliar noises. Not recognising any of the animals, I saw only glimpses of some resembling foxes, others hares, and yet more that looked like stags with impossibly curved antlers. My feet stumbled over the uneven forest floor until I found a path twisting through the trees.

I could not have walked for long when a small cottage of woven boughs appeared from the gloom. Surely whoever lived here would have seen Edward? I knocked lightly on the little door before it opened to reveal a witch, her body bent and her hair a snarled tangle. She squinted up at me with rheumy eyes.

"What brings you to my door, girl?"

"I seek my brother. He lost his shadow and walked into these woods. Do you know where he is?"

"He is not here," she harrumphed. "But if you unroll this ball of wool each day, it will lead you to the end of the world and the sorcerer who has you brother's shadow. But in return for my help, I want your beauty."

I considered her words. "I'll give you my beauty until I return this ball of wool to you."

"Agreed." She chuckled.

The witch placed a gnarled hand on my shoulder, her magic slipping over my body, scarring my face, and twisting my features until I was unrecognisable. The witch smiled with all the wholesome beauty I had possessed, and handed me the ball of wool. I clutched at the necklace I still wore; the only way Edward might still recognise me. Then I unrolled the wool and followed it from the witch's cottage.

I trekked for the full day through the Otherworld until evening drew closer; the sky going purple with the twilight. I stepped out from a dense forest into a steep gorge, granite cliffs lined with sharp crags along the top. Feeling unseen eyes upon me, I approached cautiously along the stony path through the middle of the gorge.

I had not gone far when the earth groaned in protest, boulders dislodging from the hillside and tumbling down towards me. Shrieking, I ran for the sliver of twilit sky visible between the narrow cliffs at the far end of the gorge. I had only gone a few strides when a massive form loomed in front of me. Screaming in shock, I slid to a halt in the middle of the path.

A troll blocked my escape, and I stared up at this hulking form, the muscular limbs, and blunt face. He paused, ready to crush me to pieces if I moved.

"I need passage through this gorge," I said, shaking.

"Do you now?" the troll rumbled, scratching his grey beard. "I am the guardian of this gorge, and none pass without my permission."

"I need to reach the tower at the end of the world. I will give you anything."

"The tower is just on the other side of this valley. If I let you pass, I will have your youth."

"On one condition, troll. When I return here, you will

give me back my youth.”

The troll nodded. “Agreed,” he boomed, touching one massive finger to my shoulder.

His magic was like the rock he guarded, powerful and ancient. I felt my youthful strength draining away, bending my back with age, turning my hair silver. The troll let me pass, and I shuffled through the gorge and into the hills beyond.

From the foothills, I could see the ocean and a dark stone tower perched on rocky cliffs. Beside the tower was a small cottage. Walking towards the tower, a small cottage wedged between the stone of the tower base and the ocean. Wild animals gathered around Edward while he played a flute, staring across the waves.

I wanted to run to Edward and hug him fiercely, but I still needed to bargain with the sorcerer. Staggering to the tower, its portcullis down with no one in sight, I was about to use the bell pull when a gaunt man stepped silently from the shadows nearest me.

“What brings you here?” he asked.

“I seek my brother’s shadow.”

“Very well. But in return for your brother’s shadow, I will

take away your health again."

"As long as my brother has his shadow, he can return home again."

The sorcerer smiled. "Do not tell anyone of our bargain, or the spell will be reversed."

I nodded. "Agreed."

The sorcerer plucked a shadow from his tattered robes, nimble fingers passing it to me. I recognised the slender, proud form of my brother and quickly tucked the shadow in my jacket pocket. Weaving a complex pattern in the air, the sorcerer's hands moved like a puppeteer, and I felt the familiar weakness of my sickness return. Our bargain concluded, I staggered to the little house beside the ocean, the animals all fleeing into the woods at my approach. From where he sat on a rock, Edward turned and frowned, not recognising the scarred, sick old woman I had become.

"I have something of yours," I said, releasing the shadow from my pocket. The dark shape clung to Edward's side immediately. "I bargained with the sorcerer for your shadow."

Edward's lips parted, but before he could speak, a cry of outrage was emitted from the sorcerer in the tower above.

"My sister will become sick again if I have my shadow."

"The sorcerer was greedy. He bargained your shadow away to me – I bargained my health away to him. I returned your shadow to you and you've never broken your bargain with him. I no longer have your shadow. I've broken the terms of his bargain in telling you and now my bargain with him is reversed. My health is mine again and your shadow is yours. But the sorcerer will be furious to know how he's been deceived. We must leave quickly."

"Who are you to take such risks for me?"

I touched the necklace at my throat, and Edward's eyes widened in realisation. "Emily? What have you done?"

"Nothing I can't undo on our return home. I made bargains with others along my journey."

Edward offered me his arm, and started up the agonisingly steep slope, my frail body made weaker by old age. Edward paused and played a quick trill on his flute, watching the forest with keen eyes. He had made many allies among the wild animals, and I watched in awe as a huge black stag strode from the forest. The beast stopped before me, lowering its curved antlers and dropping to its knees. Edward helped me climb onto its back and we

continued, the stag making our travel faster.

When we reached the narrow mouth of the gorge, I called to the troll. The mountainside shifted, granite grinding on granite as the troll lumbered down the steep slope, blunt face smiling.

"Emily," he said in greeting. "You got your brother's shadow back?"

"I did. Now you must uphold our bargain and return my youth to me."

The troll nodded, and careful to avoid the stag's antlers, he touched me as lightly as his huge hand could manage. Again, I felt the thrum of magic, this time filling me with energy.

"You have my blessing to pass," the troll said, grey hairs at his temples again.

Edward stared at me. I was no longer old but still made unrecognisable by the scarring to my face.

"One last bargain on our return," I said, sitting taller on the stag, healthy and young again.

We travelled the path through the forest, following its twisting bends and hollows until I saw the witch's cottage half-obscured beneath an oak tree.

"Wait here," I said to Edward, slipping from the stag's back.

Approaching the little cottage, I rapped on the front door and waited for the witch. Slowly the door opened, her beautiful face lit with surprise as she looked between me and Edward.

"You got your brother's shadow back then, girl?"

"And now our bargain must be fulfilled," I said, offering the ball of wool to her.

"Very well," she grunted, taking the wool, brushing her fingertips against my hand.

There was a rush of magic and the scars twisting my mouth and face disappeared. Hesitantly, I ran my fingers across my cheeks—my beauty had returned.

"Safe passage to you both," the witch said, closing the door before I could offer thanks.

"Our parents will be worried," Edward said.

"Then let's go home." I pulled him into a hug as he whispered a word to the black stag. The beast snorted, then disappeared back into the forest.

Following the path, we hurried through the tangle of tree branches, tripping on hidden tree roots and stones. Finally, we staggered from the forest and onto Wimbledon Common. The sun was already setting as we raced across the meadow, not looking back until we reached home.

Leanbh Pearson lives on Ngunnawal Country, in Canberra, Australia. An LGBTQI dark fiction author inspired by mythology, folklore, archaeology, history, and the environment, her short fiction features in numerous anthologies. Partially fictional, she is a keen nature and wildlife photographer, bookshop, and Museum devotee, and enjoys the Australian wilderness with her dogs (the canine assistants). Leanbh's alter-ego is an academic in archaeology and prehistory. Follow her at www.leanbhpearson.com, and on Twitter, Facebook, and Instagram @leanbhpearson.

About
Black Hare Press

lack Hare Press is a small, independent publisher based in Melbourne, Australia.

Founded in 2018, our aim has always been to champion emerging authors from all around the globe and offer opportunities for them to participate in speculative fiction and horror short story anthologies.

Connect

Website: www.blackharepress.com

Twitter: @BlackHarePress

Acknowledgements

hen we embarked on our Black Hare Press journey back in late 2018, we never envisioned the huge support we'd get from the writing community. We have been truly humbled by the number of submissions we've received.

So, thank you to everyone who crafted tales just for us—from the tiny tales in our Dark Drabbles series to these speculative stories in this 500 Fiction series—we thank you from the bottom of our hearts.

To our families and friends, collaborators, random strangers who took pity on us, and everyone who has helped us on the way: we couldn't have done it without you.

Special thanks to our Patreon supporters, especially George Wehrfritz, S. Jade Path, James Aitchison, and Jonathan Stiffy. Take a look at the Patreon-only content and merch here—patreon.com/blackharepress—and consider helping us get to the next stage.

And to you, our discerning reader, we, and these

talented writers did it all for you. We hope you enjoyed these tales, and if you did, don't forget to leave a review.

Love & kisses, the Team